Henri needed to touch her, to wrap her in his arms.

She was sexy—a tangle of tousled hair and pure fire. And in this setting—in the middle of the garden in that peach dress—she looked like a nymph those classical artists were always capturing.

He could sense the answering awareness in her, a heat she'd denied too often these past months. Now, extending a hand, he trailed it along the length of her lithe arm. Gentle pressure, the kind that used to drive her wild with anticipation. She turned to face him, leaning into his light touch.

Reaching for her hand, he threaded his fingers through hers, locking them together in that one, small way. He was holding on to her.

Could he hold on to them?

* * *

Reunited with the Rebel Billionaire is part
of the Bayou Billionaires series:
Secrets and scandal are a Cajun family legacy
for the Reynaud

D1414944

Dear Reader,

Marriage is tough. Just ask anyone who's been married. It's work when things are going well, and then when life throws in a speed bump? Holy cow, hold on for a rocky ride. Henri and Fiona Reynaud face a tremendous health challenge in their marriage and it has threatened to tear them apart. Their journey back to rediscovering love and an even stronger bond was an honor to write.

Reunited with the Rebel Billionaire is book three in the Bayou Billionaires family saga of the Reynaud brothers. And while this book stands alone as a read, I hope you'll check out all four of the stories: *His Pregnant Princess Bride* (by Catherine Mann) and *His Secretary's Surprise Fiancé* (by Joanne Rock) are both out now as well, and book four, *Secret Baby Scandal* (also by Joanne Rock), will be released in May 2016.

Joanne and I have had a blast writing about the Reynaud brothers, well-known in Louisiana, where their football exploits—whether in passing yards or in unconventional draft picks—are as much a topic of conversation as the women in their lives.

As they say in Louisiana, *"Bienvenue en Louisiane!"* ("Welcome to Louisiana!")

Cheers,

Catherine Mann

CatherineMann.com

REUNITED WITH THE REBEL BILLIONAIRE

CATHERINE MANN

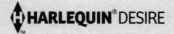

Recycling programs
for this product may
not exist in your area.

ISBN-13: 978-0-373-73454-2

Reunited with the Rebel Billionaire

Copyright © 2016 by Catherine Mann

Printed in U.S.A.

www.Harlequin.com

USA TODAY bestselling author **Catherine Mann** has penned over fifty novels, released in more than twenty countries. A RITA® Award winner, she holds a master's degree in theater and enjoys bringing that dramatic flair to her stories. Catherine and her military husband live in Florida, where they brought up their four children. Their nest didn't stay empty long, though, as Catherine is president of the Sunshine State Animal Rescue. For more information, visit catherinemann.com.

Books by Catherine Mann

HARLEQUIN DESIRE

A Christmas Baby Surprise
Sheltered by the Millionaire

Diamonds in the Rough

One Good Cowboy
Pursued by the Rich Rancher
Pregnant by the Cowboy CEO

The Alpha Brotherhood

An Inconvenient Affair
All or Nothing
Playing for Keeps
Yuletide Baby Surprise
For the Sake of Their Son

Bayou Billionaires

His Pregnant Princess Bride
Reunited with the Rebel Billionaire

Visit her Author Profile page at Harlequin.com, or catherinemann.com, for more titles!

To Dannielle—a strong, proactive survivor
with one of the most generous hearts
I've ever encountered. You inspire me.

One

Fiona Harper-Reynaud was married to *American Sports* magazine's "Hottest Athlete of the Year" for two years running.

She hadn't married the New Orleans Hurricanes' star quarterback for his looks. In fact, she'd always been drawn to the academic sort more than the jock type. But when that jock happened to be visiting an art gallery fund-raiser she'd been hosting for her father, she'd been intrigued. When Henri Reynaud had shown an appreciation and understanding of the nuances of botanic versus scenic art, she'd fallen hook, line and sinker into those dreamy, intelligent dark eyes of his. His eyes were the color of coffee and carried just as strong a jolt.

Still, she'd held back because of her own history with relationships, and yes, two broken engagements.

Held back for all of a couple of weeks. And ever since then her life hadn't stopped spiraling out of control.

Sure, they'd eloped because they'd thought she was pregnant. But she'd loved him so intensely, so passionately, reason scattered like petals from a windswept azalea. They hadn't realized until it was too late they had no substantive foundation in their marriage when difficult times came their way. And what little base they'd built upon had crumbled quickly.

Especially right now.

In two short hours, Fiona would be greeting the elite community of New Orleans for her latest fund-raiser, purely in a volunteer capacity. Any time a foundation offered to pay, she donated the funds back to the charity. She believed deeply in the causes she supported and was grateful to have the wealth and time to help.

But the pressure of the high-glitz affair wasn't what rattled her. The doctor visit today had her scared, and more determined than ever she couldn't continue a marriage built on anything but love. Certainly not built only on obligation.

She switched her phone to speaker and placed it on the antique dresser, one of many beautiful pieces in the home she shared with Henri in New Orleans's gracious and historic Garden District. Her eyes lingered on the crystal-framed photograph of her with Henri from a trip they'd taken to Paris a few years back. Their smiles caught her off guard.

Had her life ever been that happy? The version of herself in the photograph felt like a stranger now.

She'd been so focused on the photograph, she almost forgot she was on the phone with Adelaide, her future sister-in-law and longtime personal assistant to Henri's half brother Dempsey. At long last the two were engaged. Their love had taken longer to bloom, unlike Henri's impulsive proposal to Fiona.

Blinking, Fiona shifted her attention back to the conversation. To her family. She internally laughed at that thought. Family implied closeness and solidarity. Instead of that, she felt numbingly alone and isolated.

And there was no reason for that. The Reynaud family was large and the majority of them resided right here in New Orleans. Two of her husband's brothers lived in a private compound of homes on Lake Pontchartrain. And they'd be at that compound tonight for the fund-raiser.

Star athletes, celebrities and politicians would gather and mingle for Fiona's newest cause. Conversation would fill the air. And if her past events were any indication, she would raise the funds necessary to open up the new animal shelter.

She perched on the delicate Victorian settee at the end of her four-poster bed. She pulled on one thigh-high stocking as she listened to her future sister-in-law rattle off the wines, liquors and other beverages delivered.

Still caught in the past, when she'd fallen hard for Henri Reynaud, she rolled the silk socking up her other leg. Henri had chased her relentlessly until she'd begun to believe him when he said he adored her mind every bit as much as her body.

Her body.

Hands shaking, she tugged the band on her thigh into place. She couldn't afford to think about those days before their marriage turned rocky, only to have him stay with her because of her health. She respected his honor, even as it hurt her to the core to lose his love. But she couldn't accept anything less than honest emotion.

Which meant she had to keep her secret. She tugged a wrinkle from her stocking and continued her phone conversation with Adelaide. "I can't thank you enough for helping me out with tonight's fund-raiser."

"Glad to lend my help. I wish you would ask more often."

"I didn't want to impose or make you feel pressured before when Dempsey was your boss." She'd known Adelaide for years, but only recently had they all learned of her romance with Dempsey Reynaud.

"But now that we're going to be sisters-in-law, I'm fair game?"

"Oh, um, I'm sorry." Her mind was so jumbled today. "I didn't mean that the way it came out."

"No need to apologize," Adelaide said, laughing softly. "Truly. I was just teasing. I'm really glad to lend a hand. It's a great cause. You do so much for charity—it's an inspiration."

"Well, I would have been an inspiring failure if not for your help today setting up the party at the compound." The main family compound on Lake Pontchartrain was larger and more ornate than Fiona and Henri's personal getaway. They'd purchased the place for privacy, a space she could decorate in her own antique, airy style in contrast to the palatial Greek Revival and Italianate mansions that made up the bulk of the family compound. She was grateful for the privacy right now as she readied herself for the party and steadied her nerves.

"Emergencies crop up for everyone. Did you sort

things out with your car?" Traces of concern laced Adelaide's voice.

Fiona winced. She didn't like lying to people, but if she admitted to seeing the doctor today that would trigger questions she was still too shaken to answer. After years of fertility treatments, she was used to keeping her medical history and heartbreak secret. "All is well, Adelaide. Thank you."

Or at least she hoped all was well. The doctor told her she shouldn't worry.

Easier said than done after all she had been through. Worrying had become her natural state, her automatic reflex lately.

"Glad to hear it. I emailed you the changes made to the menu so you can cross-check with the receipts."

"Changes?" Anxiety coiled in Fiona's chest. Normally she rolled with last-minute changes. They presented her with an opportunity to become more creative in the execution of the event. Every event she'd ever run had called for an adjustment or two. But her mind was elsewhere and her deeply introspective state made dealing with these external changes difficult.

"There were some last-minute problems with getting fresh mushrooms, so I made substitutions. Do you want me to go over them now?" Keys clicked in the background.

"Of course not. I trust your taste and experience." And she did.

"If you need my help with anything else, let me know." Adelaide hesitated until the sound of someone else speaking then leaving the room faded. "I'm comfortable in my work world, but my future role and

responsibilities as a Reynaud spouse will be new ter-
ritory to me."

And Fiona's time as a Reynaud wife was drawing
to an end, even if the family didn't know it yet. Her
heart sank. "You are a professional at this. You could
take any event to a whole new level. Just make sure to
find what you want your niche to be. The men in this
family can steamroll right over a person." The words
tumbled out of her mouth, and her cool, collected front
began to crumble.

"Fiona…" Concern tinged her voice. "Are you okay?"

"Don't mind me. I'm fine. I'll see you soon. I need
to get changed." She couldn't attend the event in stockings, a thong and a bra. No matter how fine the im-
ported Italian lace. "Thanks again." She disconnected
and slid her sapphire-blue gown from the end of the
bed.

She stepped into the floor-length dress, the silk chiffon a cool glide over her skin, the dress and underwear
strategically designed. The fabric fit snugly in a swathe
around her breasts and hips, with a looser pleated skirt
grazing her ankles. A sequin-studded belt complemented her glinting diamond chandelier earrings.

No one would see her scars. No one other than her
husband and doctors knew.

Double mastectomy.

Reconstruction.

Prophylactic—preventative. In hopes of evading
the disease that had claimed her mother, her aunt and
her grandmother.

Fiona had never had breast cancer. But with her genetics, she couldn't afford to take the risk. She pressed
the dress to her chest and tried not to think of the

doctor's words today about a suspicious reading on her breast MRI that could be nothing. The doctor said the lump was almost certainly benign fat necrosis. But just to be safe he wanted to biopsy...

The creaking of the opening door startled her. Her dress slid down and she grabbed it by the embellished straps, pressing it back to her chest even though she knew only one person would walk in unannounced.

Her husband.

America's hottest athlete for two years running.

And the man she hadn't slept with since her surgery six months ago.

Henri's hands fell to rest on her shoulders, his breath caressing her neck. "Need help with the zipper?"

Henri took risks in his job on a regular basis. Sure, his teammates worked their asses off to prevent a hard tackle from his blind side, but he understood and accepted that every time he stepped onto the field, he could suffer a career-ending injury.

Fans called him brave. Sports analysts sometimes labeled him reckless. The press branded him fearless.

They were all wrong.

He'd been scared as hell every day since the doctors declared Fiona had inherited her family's cancer gene. It didn't matter that their marriage had been on the rocks. He'd been rocked to his foundation. Still was.

Henri clenched her shoulders so his hands wouldn't shake. Even the smallest touch between them was filled with tension. And not in the way that made him weak in the knees. "Your zipper?"

With a will of their own, his eyes took in the long exposed line of her neck, her deep brown hair corralled by a thin braid so that lengthy, loose curls cascaded in a narrow path down her back. He looked farther down her spine to the small of her back that called to him to touch, to kiss in a lingering, familiar way. But he'd lost the right. She'd made that clear when he'd tried to reconcile after the doctor's prognosis.

"Thank you. Yes, please," she said, glancing over her shoulder nervously and pulling her hair aside, the strands so dark they almost appeared black at night. He hated seeing that sort of distance in her amber-colored eyes. "I'm running late because of, um, a last-minute snafu with the caterer."

"Adelaide said you were having trouble with your car, so I came home early. But I see it's in the garage. What was wrong?"

Whipping her head away from his gaze, she muttered, "Doesn't matter."

It was becoming her trademark response. It didn't matter.

That was a lie. He could tell by the way her mouth thinned as she spoke.

He let out a deep sigh as his gaze traced over their room. Or should he say—their *former* room. He'd taken to sleeping in the guest bedroom of the restored home. Away from her. They'd even lost the ability to lie next to each other at night. To show up for each other in that simple way.

In front of him was the first gift he'd ever bought Fiona. It was a handsome jewelry armoire that doubled as a full-length mirror. It was a one-of-a-kind antique piece. Whimsical and light. Just like Fiona in her jewel-colored dress. Looking at the gilded mirror framing the reflection of his exquisite wife reminded him of how far they'd fallen. Damn.

This whole room was a mausoleum to what had been.

He wanted her to lean on him. Even if it was just a little bit. This wasn't what he wanted. "Anything else I can do to help?"

"I've got it under control." Finality colored her words.

"You always do." It came out harsher than he intended. But dammit, he was trying. Couldn't she see that?

She spun around to face him, her petite frame filling with rigid rage as the silk of her gown whirled against his shins. Raising her chin and her brow, she pressed her lips tight, primly. "No need to be snarky."

Sticking his hands in his pants pockets, he shrugged, his Brioni tuxedo jacket sliding along his shoulders. "I am completely serious."

Fiona's sherry eyes softened, the amber depths intoxicating. She took a deep breath and stared at him. A breeze stirred the stale air of the room, filtering through the window with the sounds of foot traffic and car horns. It was a grounding sound, reminding him of when they'd first bought this house—when they'd been a team. They'd spent months working together on every detail of restoring the historic Victorian home, a celebrated building that had once been a schoolhouse, then a convent.

And they'd done it together. They'd transformed this deteriorating five-thousand-square-foot house into a home.

"Sorry, I didn't mean to start a fight. Adelaide was

a huge help during a really long day. Let's just get through the evening. It's harder and harder to pretend there's nothing wrong between us."

Something was off with her today, but he couldn't tell what. It was clear enough, though, that she was trying to pick a fight with him.

"I don't want to fight with you, either." He didn't know what the hell he wanted anymore other than to have things the way they were.

"You used to love a good argument with me. Only me. You get along with everyone else. I never understood that."

"We had fire, you and I." It had been a sizzling love. One that warmed him to his damn core. And he knew there was still a spark in the embers. He couldn't believe it was all gone.

"Had, Henri. That's my point. It's over, and you need to quit making excuses to delay the final step." Ferocity returned to her fairylike features. A warrior in blue silk and sequins.

"Not excuses. You needed to recover. Then we agreed we wouldn't do anything that would disrupt the start of the season. Then with my brother's wedding on the horizon—"

"Excuses. Divorce isn't the end of the world." She pinned up a curl that had escaped the confines of the delicate braid binding the others into place.

Everything about her these days was carefully put together so that no one saw a hint of the turmoil beneath. For months he'd respected that. Understood she was the one calling the shots with her health issues. But how could she deny herself any help? Ever? She'd made it clear he didn't know how to be the least bit of assistance.

And now, divorce was the recurring refrain.

"Our family is in the spotlight. A split between us would eat up positive oxygen in the press." He needed her to take a deep breath. They needed to figure out everything. He needed to stall.

She turned back around, using the mirror to smooth her dress. "No one is going to think poorly of you for leaving me. I will make it clear I'm the one who asked for the divorce."

Anger boiled, heating his cheeks. "I don't give a damn what people think about me."

"But you do care about your team. I understand." He picked up on the implication of her words. That he didn't care about *her*. And that couldn't be farther off base. She was still trying to pick a fight. To widen the gap between them.

"We're going to be late." The tone of his voice was soft. Almost like a whisper. He wanted to calm her down, to stop this from turning into an unnecessary fight. Something was upsetting her. Something major.

As much as he wanted to understand her, he couldn't. The party was about to start and he didn't have the time to unwrap the subtle meaning of all her words.

All he wanted was to have their old life back instead of silently cohabitating and putting on a front for the world. He longed for her to look at him the way she used to, with that smile that said as much as she enjoyed the party, she savored their time alone together even more. He ached for their relationship to be as uncomplicated as it once was when they traveled the country for the season, traveled the world in the off-season. They both enjoyed history and art. Sightseeing on hikes, whether to see Stonehenge or the Great Wall of China.

Tapping the back of her dress, he met her gaze in the mirror, holding her tawny eyes and reveling in the way her pupils widened with unmistakable desire. Settling his hands back on her shoulders, he breathed against her ear and neck. "Unless you would like me to take the zipper back down again."

Her lashes fluttered shut for a second and a softness entered her normally clenched jaw. In that brief moment, he thought this might be how they closed the gap.

Instead, her eyelids flew open and she shimmied out from underneath his hands. "No, thank you. I have a fund-raiser to oversee. And then make no mistake, we need to set a firm date to see our attorney and end the marriage."

Two

Fiona picked at sequins on her dress as Henri steered their Maserati through the gates and toward the huge Greek Revival mansion on the hill. She'd lived just down the road from that house once, she and Henri in their wing and his youngest brother, Jean-Pierre, in another. Both wings were large enough for privacy. Both easily big enough to fit four of the homes she'd grown up in, and her family had been wealthy enough to impress, with her father owning a midsize accounting firm.

But once her honeymoon phase had worn off with Henri and she'd realized she wasn't pregnant, they'd begun trying for a baby in earnest. That mammoth mansion had grown more claustrophobic with each failed attempt. Then with each fertility treatment. There'd been miscarriages they hadn't even told the family about. So many more health heartaches they hadn't shared with his family.

After her very public miscarriage in her second trimester, he'd bought them the house in the Garden District to give them both space from the Reynaud fishbowl lifestyle. Their emotions had been bubbling over far too often, in good and bad ways.

Living here? It was just too difficult. Spanish moss trailed like bridal veils from live oak trees on either side of the private driveway leading into the Reynaud estate on Lake Pontchartrain. It was in an exclusive section of Metairie, Louisiana, west of the city. Pontoon boats were moored in shallow waters while long docks stretched into the low-lying mist that often settled on the surface, sea grass spiking through and hiding local creatures. The gardens were lush and verdant, the ground fertile. Gardeners had to work overtime to hold back the Louisiana undergrowth that could take over in no time. The place was large, looming—alive.

She glanced at her too-damn-handsome husband as he steered their sports car up the winding drive toward the original home on the family complex, the place where Henri and his brothers had spent time in their youth. Gervais, the oldest brother, and his fiancée lived here now, and the couple had allowed Fiona to host her event on the property.

Henri's tailored Brioni tuxedo fit his hard, muscled body well. His square jaw was cleanly shaved, his handsome face the kind that could have graced a *GQ* cover. Her attraction to him hadn't changed, but so much had shifted between them since their impulsive elopement three years ago. While she didn't care about missing out on a large wedding, she did wonder if things might have turned out differently if they'd waited longer, gotten to know each other better before the stress piled on.

Now they would never know.

He bypassed the valet and opted to park in the family garage. The steel door slid open to reveal a black Range Rover and a Ferrari facing forward, shiny with polish, grills glistening. He backed into an open space, the massive garage stretching off to the side filled with recreational vehicles. The boats and Jet Skis were down in the boathouse at the dock. This family loved their toys. They played hard. Lived large. And loved full-out.

Losing Henri already left a hole in her life. Losing this family would leave another.

She swallowed down a lump as the garage door slid closed and he shut off the vehicle.

"Fiona?" He thumbed the top of the steering wheel. "Thank you for keeping up the happy couple act in public. I know things haven't been easy between us."

"This fund-raiser means a lot to me."

"Of course it does." His mouth went tight and she realized she'd hurt him.

How could they be so certain things were over and still have the power to hurt each other with a stray word? "I appreciate that your connections make this possible."

He glanced at her, smoothing his lapel. "You throw a great party that wins over a crowd not easily wowed."

"I owe Adelaide for her help today."

"When your car broke down."

She nodded tightly, the lie sticking in her throat.

He reached out to touch a curl and let it loosely wrap

around his finger as if with a will of its own. "You look incredible tonight. Gorgeous."

"Thank you."

"Any chance you're interested in indulging in some make-up sex, even if only temporary?"

The offer was tempting, mouthwateringly so, as she took in the sight of her husband's broad shoulders, was seduced by the gentle touch of his fingers rubbing just one curl.

"We need to get inside."

His mocha-colored eyes lingered on her mouth as tangibly as any kiss, setting her senses on fire. "Of course. Just know the offer stands."

He winked before smoothly sliding out of the car and moving around to the passenger side with the speed and grace that served him well on the ball field. Her skin still tingled from the thought of having sex with him again. They'd been so very good together in bed, with a chemistry that was off the charts.

Would that change because of her surgery? It was a risk she'd never been able to bring herself to take.

Just the thought had her gut knotting with nerves. But the next thing she knew, her silver Jimmy Choo heels were clicking along to the side entrance and across the foyer's marble floors. The space was filled with people from corner to corner, chatter and music from the grand piano echoing up to the high ceiling. The party was in full swing. The place was packed, people standing so close together they were pushed up against walls with hand-painted murals depicting a fox hunt.

Once upon a time she'd lived for these parties. But right now, she wanted to grab the banister and run up the huge staircase with a landing so large it fit a small sofa for casual chitchat in the corner.

Her hand tucked in Henri's arm, she went on autopilot party mode, nodding and answering people's greetings. She and Henri had played this game often, fooling others. She had to admit that while women chased him unabashedly, his gaze never strayed. He was a man of honor. His father's infidelities had left a mark on him. Henri had made it clear he would never cheat—even when the love had left their marriage.

No, she couldn't let her thoughts go there. To the end of love and of them. At least, not while they were in public. Too many people were counting on her. While planning this fund-raiser had served as a distraction from the widening gap between her and Henri, the whole event still had to be properly executed.

Time to investigate her handiwork. Excusing herself, Fiona walked over to the favor table. Turquoise boxes with silver calligraphic font reading "Love at First Woof" lined the table. Laughing inwardly, she picked up one of the boxes. This one was wrapped in a white ribbon. She opened the box, pleased to find the pewter dog earrings staring back at her. Satisfied, she retied the bow, set the box on the table, and picked up a box wrapped with black ribbon. To her relief, the pewter paw tie tacks were in there, as well. Good. The favors were even cuter than she had remembered.

Fiona's gaze flicked to the service dogs from a rescue organization. They sat at attention, eyes watchful and warm. Glancing over her shoulder, she saw the plates of food in the dining room. People were gathered around the food, scooping crab cakes and chicken skewers onto their plates.

Convinced that everything was more than in order, she surveyed further, walking into a more casual family space with an entertainment bar and Palladian windows overlooking the pool and grounds.

No detail had been missed thanks to the highly efficient catering staff she'd hired and Adelaide had overseen. Smiling faintly, Fiona peered outside at the twinkling doghouse situated just beyond the luxurious in-ground pool. The doghouse was a scale replica of the Reynaud mansion, and it was going to the shelter after tonight. But for now, it lit the grounds and housed hand-painted water bowls for the shelter dogs. Four of the shelter dogs walked around the pool, enjoying all the attention and affection from the guests.

People were spread out. Laughter floated on the breeze, and so did snippets of conversation. A small Jack Russell terrier was lazily stretched on Mrs. Daniza's lap. A fuzzy white dog was curled up, fast asleep, beneath Jack Rani's chair. The dogs were winning over friends with deep pockets.

Everything appeared to be in order. But then again, Fiona knew firsthand the difference between appearances and actual reality.

Sadness washed over her. Grabbing a glass of water from a nearby beverage station, she continued on as Henri went to speak to his brothers. Movement was good. Movement was necessary. The busier she stayed, the less her emotions would sting through her veins.

And it was as if the world knew she needed a distraction. As she slipped out onto the pool deck, she saw two of her favorite Hurricanes' players—wide receiver "Wild Card" Wade and "Freight Train" Freddy. Not only did they inspire her with how much of their time they donated to worthwhile causes, the two men always made her laugh.

It seemed that tonight would be no exception. Freight Train was in a black suit, but his tie had dog butts all over it and his belt buckle was a silver paw print. He and Wild Card were posing for pictures with two of the shelter dogs. Their energy was contagious.

Directly across from Freight Train and Wild Card were the Texas branch of the Reynaud clan. When fund-raisers or troubles arose, despite the complicated and sometimes strained relationships, they jumped in. The two Texas boys were sipping wine and talking to a Louisiana senator. The cousins were supporting their relative who played for the Hurricanes. Brant Reynaud wore his ever-present small yellow rosebud on his lapel.

Everyone was out in full force to support her latest cause. She would miss this sense of family.

Landscape lighting highlighted ornamental plantings and statues. She checked the outdoor kitchen to one side of the pool to make sure all was in order. The hearth area was unmistakably popular, a fire already ablaze in the stone surround. Built-in stone seating was covered with thick cushions and protected by a pergola with a casual wrought-iron framework. The Reynaud brothers were there. Well, at least two of them. Fiona watched as Gervais waved Henri over.

One of the things that amused Fiona was the sheer amount of posturing the boys did when they were around each other. They loved each other—there was no doubt about that. But the brothers were all driven and natural-born competitors.

They were all tall, with athletic builds, dark eyes

and even darker hair, thick and lush. While Gervais, Henri and Jean-Pierre were full brothers, Dempsey was the result of one of their father's affairs. The brothers had each gotten their mother's hair coloring, while their father had donated his size and strength.

The semicircle of the Reynaud clan was an elegant one. Gervais, the most refined of the brothers, was at ease in his role as oldest, leader of the pack. Erika, his fiancée, laid a gentle hand on Gervais's forearm as she leaned into the conversation. The light from the hearth caught on her silver rings and cushion-cut diamond engagement ring. One would likely never guess Erika had served in her home country's military, although her princess bearing was entirely clear.

To Gervais's immediate left stood Dempsey, ever-present football pin on the lapel of his tuxedo, with lovely, efficient Adelaide at his side.

Fiona told herself that she was lucky not to have to work. That she made a positive impact in the world with her volunteer philanthropic efforts. Not holding down a regular job outside the home also enabled her to travel with her husband. She helped organize outings for the other family members who traveled with the Hurricanes, as well. Keeping the players and their families happy kept the team focused and out of trouble.

She looked around at the packed event, a total success. Anyone would think she had a full life.

Except she couldn't bring herself to have sex with her husband. She'd been so certain the surgery was the right decision. She'd gone to counseling before and after. Her husband had been completely supportive.

And still the distance between them had grown wider and wider these past months, emphasizing how little they knew about each other. They'd married because of infatuation, great sex, a shared love of art and a pregnancy scare that sped up the wedding date.

Now that the initial glow of infatuation had passed and they didn't even have sex to carry them through the rough patches, a common love for gallery showings wasn't enough to hold them together. Their marriage was floundering. Badly. She needed to keep in mind how dangerous it would be to let her guard down around a man who had worked hard to take care of her through her decision.

And with a cancer scare looming over her today, she couldn't bear the thought that he would stay with her out of sympathy.

Henri wasn't in much of a party mood, no matter how much his brothers elbowed him and teased him about his latest fumble. His Texas cousins weren't cutting him any slack, either.

He'd been thinking about the divorce his wife insisted on pursuing.

While the love had left their marriage, he'd heard plenty say that marriage had ups and downs. He wasn't a quitter. And damn it all, he still burned to have her.

His gaze skimmed the guests around the pool, landing on his wife. Her trailing curls and slim curves called to him, reminding him of the enticing feel of her back as he'd tugged her zipper up.

She smiled at whomever she spoke to—a man with his back to the rest of the crowd—and nodded as she walked away. The man turned and Henri's breath froze in his chest. He knew the man well. Dr. Carlson was a partner in the practice Fiona used to see before they'd transferred her to another physician for the surgery.

Fear jelling in his gut, Henri charged away from his brothers and cousins, shouldering through the crowd to his wife.

"Henri—"

He grasped her arm and guided her toward the shore of Lake Pontchartrain. "In a moment. When no one can overhear us."

Lights from yachts and boats dotted the distance. Along the shoreline, couples walked hand in hand. Henri opened the boathouse door and stepped inside. Moonlight streaked through the windows, across Fiona's face. Confusion and frustration stamped her lovely features.

He angled them beneath a pontoon boat on a lift. The boat was still wet from use, and water tapped the ground in a rhythm that almost matched his pounding heart. Inhaling deeply, he caught the musty scent of the boathouse mixed with the cinnamon notes of Fiona's perfume. He'd bought it for her on a trip to France before all of these difficulties had really gotten out of control.

"Enough already, Henri. Would you please tell me why we're out here?"

He clasped both of her shoulders. "Are you okay?"

"What do you mean?"

"I saw you talking to Dr. Carlson." He looked in her sherry-colored eyes, trying to read her. Something flickered there, something he could have sworn was fear, but then she looked away, her lashes shielding her expression.

Staring at the floor, she chewed her bottom lip for

an instant before answering, "We were discussing a fund-raiser and party for the pediatric oncology ward. The planner had a heart attack and they need someone to step in and help."

Okay, but why was she looking away? "You're sure that's all?"

She hesitated a second too long. "What do you mean?"

Fear exploded inside him. "Are you feeling all right?" He clasped her shoulders. "Physically. Is there something wrong? If so, you know I'm here for you. Whatever you need, just tell me."

She squeezed her eyes closed, shaking her head, tears sliding free.

He reached to sketch his knuckles along her cheeks and capture the tears, hands shaking. "Oh, God, Fiona, is it..." His throat moved in a long swallow. "Do you have..."

She touched his mouth. "You don't have to worry about me. I'm fine. Thank you, but you have no reason to feel obligated."

"Obligated?" He kissed her fingertips. "You are my wife, my responsibility—"

"Please, Henri." She took his hands from her face and clasped them briefly before letting go. "You are a good man. I've never doubted that. This is an emotional time for both of us, and let's not make it worse with confrontations. Let's just return to the party."

He wouldn't be dismissed so easily. "What were you laughing so hysterically about?" Anger edged through the fear. "And would you like to clue me in on the joke? Because right now I could use something to lighten the mood."

"No joke," she said with a sigh, meeting his gaze. "Just so ironic."

"Then what are you hiding?"

"Henri." She chewed her bottom lip again, her gaze skipping around evasively before she continued. "Um, he asked me out for a drink to discuss the fund-raiser."

Henri saw red. Pure red. "He asked you out for a drink? As in a date? Not because of the fund-raiser?"

"Because of the fund-raiser, but yes, he clearly meant a date, as well." She pulled at her curls, color mounting in her cheeks.

Henri had to stay calm. Had to make it through this conversation. "And what did you say?"

"I told him I'm still married, of course." Gaze narrowing, she launched the words at him like daggers.

"Clearly that wasn't a problem for him, since you are wearing my ring."

She shrugged her shoulders, chandelier earrings swaying. "That didn't bother him in the least."

Henri turned toward the door, ready to return to the party and deck the guy straight into the pool.

Fiona placed a hand on his shoulder. "Stop, Henri. He mentioned hearing we're splitting up. He thought I was available."

"How would he have heard such a thing?" His mind went back to the original concern. "Were you at the doctor's office where he's a partner?"

She swallowed hard. "You seem to have forgotten his brother is our lawyer."

"Not anymore."

"I was thinking the same thing, actually." She picked at her French manicure. "We should get separate attorneys."

Dammit. This conversation was not going the way he intended. He just wanted to pull her into his arms and take her here. Now. To say to hell with the past and future. No more jealousy or discussion about…hell.

He just wanted her. "This is not the time or the place to talk about lawyers. Enjoy your party and your success." He cupped her face in his hands, his thumbs stroking along her cheeks as he stepped closer, the heat of her lithe body reaching to him. "You've raised enough seed money for the shelter tonight. They can start their capital campaign for a whole new building. Let's celebrate."

She swayed toward him for an instant, as if she too was caught in that same web of desire. Her gaze fell away from his for a moment, roving his broad-shouldered body, then returned to meet his hungry gaze. There was something there still. He could feel it in the way her lips, slightly parted, seemed to call him to her.

Stepping back abruptly, she grasped the door latch. "Enjoy?" She shook her head, a curl sliding forward over her shoulder. "I don't think that's possible. There's too much left unsettled for me to think about anything but getting my life in order."

In a swirl of French perfume, she walked out the door and raced along the dock back to the party. The forcefulness of her reaction left him wondering what he was missing, but the speed of her departure closed the door on finding out.

She couldn't go back to the party. Not with her emotions in such a turmoil. She hadn't expected the brief conversation with Tom Carlson to lead to a showdown with her husband. But Tom had seen her come through the office earlier…and he had asked her for a drink. She'd shut him down hard. Even if she weren't married, she was not in a place emotionally to be in a relationship right now.

Life was getting too complicated. She longed for simpler times again.

Peace.

Family.

So she sought out the last remnants. She loaded a plate of party food onto a tray with two glasses of mint iced tea and went upstairs to Grandpa Leon's suite. His Alzheimer's had progressed to the point that he required a round-the-clock nurse to keep watch over him so he didn't wander off. His nighttime nurse's aide sat in the study area off his bedroom, reading on her phone. A brunette in her midthirties, she had a warm expression on her face at all times. The perfect temperament for at-home care.

She looked up quickly and set her phone beside her. "Good evening, Mrs. Reynaud. Mr. Leon is on the balcony enjoying the stars over the lake."

They'd glassed in the balcony so the temperature could be regulated year-round, and he could safely sit outside without fear of him falling—or climbing down as he'd tried to do one evening.

"Thank you," Fiona said. "Please do feel free to join the party while I visit with Gramps."

"That sounds lovely. Thank you. I'll step downstairs for a snack. I'll be back in a half hour, if that's all right?"

"Absolutely. Take your time." Fiona loved her grandfather-in-law and treasured this time with him.

His disease was stealing him away and she would soon be gone. Her heart squeezed tighter as she stepped through the open French doors leading to the enclosed balcony.

"Grandpa Leon," she said softly, adjusting the tray and settling it on the wrought-iron table between two chairs. "I've brought you a bite to eat."

The older man turned, his shock of gray hair whiter every day as if each lost memory stole more of his youth along with the color in the once dark strands. "They don't like me going to parties anymore. I believe they're afraid of what I might say."

"Everyone loves having you there. I'm sorry you feel that way, though." The family was just trying to protect him from embarrassment.

"It's not your fault my memory's failing. The boys are just trying to protect me and my pride." Spearing a bit of shrimp scampi on his fork, he looked up at her gratefully. "This is good, especially for party food. Filling. Not a bunch of those frilly little canapés."

"We have plenty of those, too. I just know your preference."

"And I appreciate that. My tastes are the only thing not failing in my mind. But I imagine you knew that. You were always a perceptive girl. I am going to miss you."

Her head jerked up. What did he know? He couldn't possibly have guessed about the divorce. "Grandpa Leon, I'm not sure what you mean."

He tapped his temple. "When my illness takes over. Even in my fog, I feel the sense of loss. I feel it here." He tapped his chest. "The people who should be a part of my life. But I can't recall who belongs to me and who doesn't."

Fiona didn't even know what to say, so she covered his hand with hers and squeezed. "I do love you and I won't forget you."

"And I love you, too, sister dear."

She blinked away a tear. She shouldn't be surprised any longer at these moments he mistook her for someone else. Still… She shoved to her feet and started for the door.

Turning to look back at the man who soon wouldn't be her grandfather anymore, Fiona said, "Do you want seconds on anything?"

He stared back at her, a confused look in his java-brown eyes. "Seconds?" He stared down at his empty plate. "What did the chef make for dinner? I can't seem to recall."

She struggled for what to say and then realized specifics didn't matter so much as peace. "Tonight's menu included your very favorite."

He smiled, passing his plate to her. "Of course, my favorite. I would like more. And dessert—pie with ice cream."

"Of course."

Would he even remember he'd asked for it when she returned? She would bring it all the same and savor her last moments as part of this wonderful family.

Would she still be welcome here to visit him after the split became known to the rest of the family? Would she even be able to come here without losing her mind? The pain would be…intense. Especially at first. And later? She could barely think into the future. She'd been so afraid to dream years ahead for fear there were no years for her.

Today had reminded her all too well of those fears.

Three

Always hungry—which was the fate of an athlete—
Henri pulled open the door to the Sub-Zero fridge,
rummaging around shelves big enough to park a car—
his personal choice in the kitchen remodel. It was three
in the morning and no way would he make it until
dawn. Though the food at the party had been deca-
dent, he needed to put proper fuel into his system. In
season, he put his body through the wringer and there
was a helluva lot at stake.

He pulled out a carton of eggs and placed them on
the granite counter. Running a hand through his hair,
his mind drifted back to the fund-raiser.

From an outside perspective, the event was a complete success. Seven figures had been raised, more
than enough seed money to launch a capital campaign
to build a new shelter. His wife's fund-raising goal

had been surpassed. And he was damn proud of her. Even if things were difficult right now, he admired her spirit. He'd practically had to drag her out of the fund-raiser as the cleanup crews arrived. Fiona had wanted to make sure that everything was perfect, that things were easy on the housekeeping staff.

Of course, by the time they'd returned to their house, she'd bolted from his company and retreated to her room. Par for the course these days.

Opening a cabinet drawer, he pulled out a frying pan and sprayed it with olive oil. He switched on the gas of the massive gourmet cooktop and adjusted the flame. Once the pan began to hiss to life, he cracked two eggs, reveling in the sound and the promise of protein.

Cooking was one of the things that he actually liked to do for himself. And for Fiona. He'd made them delicious, flavorful and healthy meals. That was one of the reasons they'd spent so much time restoring this kitchen. It had been a space where they had bonded.

They had jointly picked the decorations in the room, visiting high-end antiques stores in the French Quarter and finding beautiful pieces. Like the big turn-of-the-century clock that occupied a prominent spot on the south wall. The clock was an intricate work of angles and loops. The antique vibe of the wrought iron had reminded them both of Ireland, which was one of the first places they'd traveled to together.

The room contained an eclectic mix of items—nothing matched, but the pieces complemented each other, pulling the room together.

With a sigh, he slid the eggs out of the pan and onto a plate. After he'd fumbled in the drawer for a fork, he grabbed the plate and made his way to the large window in the dining room. He sat at the head of the long cherrywood table, bought for entertaining the whole family. A gilded mirror hung over the sideboard laden with Fiona's well-polished silver. Even though they'd built this haven together, if they split, he would be booted out on his ass and moving back to the family compound with his brothers. He loved his family, but this place was home now, deep in the heart of New Orleans.

The thought of leaving made it too damn hard to sit at this table—their table. Pushing his plate of half-eaten eggs away, he shot to his feet and wandered to the window.

Sometimes the contrasts of this city just struck him, the historic buildings jutting up against contemporary trends. It was a place between worlds and cultures. The New Orleans moon hung in the late night sky, just peeking through sullen clouds that covered the stars. He'd always enjoyed the moodiness of this place, his new home after growing up in Texas. This fit his personality, his temperament. He'd thought he had his life together when he met Fiona. Perfect wife. Dream career. Jazz music that could wake the dead and reach a cold man's soul.

His brothers would laugh at him for saying stuff like that, call him a sensitive wuss, but Fiona had understood the side of him that enjoyed art and music. It cut him deep that she said they didn't know each other, that they had no foundation and nothing in common.

She minimized what they'd built together, and that sliced him to the core. It hadn't helped one bit that men were hitting on her at the party, already sensing a divorce in the wind even if they hadn't announced it to a soul.

He was used to men approaching his wife. She was drop-dead gorgeous in a chic and timeless way that would draw attention for the rest of her life. But tonight had been different. He spent so much time on the road and she usually traveled with him. But even when they weren't together, they'd always trusted each other. The thought of her moving on, of her with another man, shredded him inside. He didn't consider himself the jealous type, but he damn well wasn't ready to call it quits and watch her move on with someone—anyone—else.

Without his realizing it, his feet carried him past the window, past the living room. And suddenly, he was upstairs outside Fiona's room.

Her door was wide open. That was the first thing that jarred him. He'd become so accustomed to seeing that closed door when he passed by her room at night. Fiona had literally shut him out.

So why was it open tonight?

Not that he was going to miss the opportunity to approach her.

The soft, warm light from her bedroom bathed the hall in a yellow glow. Curiosity tugged at him, and he peered into the room.

She was curled up in a tight ball on the settee at the foot of the bed, her sequined waistband expanding and contracting with her slow, determined breaths. He was surprised to see her still in her party clothes. Even with disheveled, wavy hair she was damn breathtaking. Her shoes were casually and chaotically tossed to the side.

For a moment, he thought she was asleep, and then he realized...

Fiona was crying.

A rush of protectiveness pulsed through his body. Fiona had been so calculating and logical these days that this spilling of emotion overwhelmed him. Damn, he didn't want to see her like this. He *never* wanted to see her like this. It made him feel helpless, and that was a feeling he'd never handled well.

Once when Henri was younger, he'd walked into his mother's room to find her crying. Tears had streaked her face, mascara marring her normally perfect complexion. She had been crying over the death of her career as a model. And his father's infidelity. She'd been so shattered, and all Henri could do was watch from the sidelines.

She hadn't been the most attentive or involved parent, but she'd been his mother and he'd wanted to make the world right for her.

He'd felt every bit as useless then as he felt now.

"Fiona?" He stepped tentatively into the room.

Startled, she sat up, dragging her wrist across her tears and smudging mascara into her hairline. "Henri, I don't need help with my zipper."

"I was on my way to my room and I heard you." He stepped deeper into the room, tuxedo jacket hooked on one finger and slung over his shoulder. "Are you okay?"

"No, I'm not," she said in a shaky voice, swinging her bare feet to the floor and digging her toes into the wool Persian rug they'd chosen together at an estate auction.

Something was different about her today. She was

showing a vulnerability around him, an openness, he hadn't seen in nearly a year. And that meant there was still something salvageable between them.

For the first time in a long time, they were actually talking, and he wasn't giving up that window of opportunity to figure out what was going on in her mind. He didn't know where they were going, but he sure as hell wasn't willing to just write off what they'd had. "It's tougher and tougher to be together in front of people and pretend. I get that. Totally. That's what you're upset about, isn't it?"

"Of course," she answered too quickly.

"Why am I having trouble believing you?" He draped his jacket over a wing-back chair by the restored fireplace. "We didn't have trouble with trust before."

"It's easy to trust when you don't know each other well, when we kept our life superficial." The words came out of her mouth almost like lines from a play. Too calculated, too rehearsed.

He leaned back against the marble mantel. "You're going to have to explain that to me, because I'm still bemused as hell as to where we went wrong."

Sighing, she smoothed the silk dress over her knees. "We forgot to talk about the important things, like what would happen if we couldn't have kids. What we would have bonding us besides having lots of sex and procreating."

Sifting through her explanation, he tried to make sense of her conflicting signals, her words and body language and nervous twitches all at odds. "You only saw sex between us as about having children? Is that why you've been pushing me away since your mastectomy and hysterectomy?" Because of the genetic testing, the doctor had recommended both, and Henri hadn't been able to deny the grief they'd both felt over the end to any chance of conceiving a child together. But the bottom line was, he'd cared most about keeping his wife alive. "You know I'm here for you, no matter what. I'm not going to leave you when you need me."

Her expression was shuttered, her emotions hidden again. "We've discussed this. Without kids, we have nothing holding us together."

Nothing except for their passion, their shared interests. Their shared life. She couldn't be willing to discount that so quickly.

"And you're still against adoption?" He was stumped about that, considering her father was adopted. But she'd closed down when he brought up the subject.

"I'm against a man staying with me for the children or out of sympathy because he thinks I'm going to die." She shot to her feet, a coolness edging her features. "Could we please stop this discussion, dammit?"

Was that what she thought? That he had only stayed because of her cancer gene? They'd discussed divorce before then, but only briefly. After? She'd dug in her heels about the split.

He couldn't deny he wouldn't have left a woman facing the possibility of a terminal illness, but their relationship was more complex than that. He shoved away from the fireplace strewn with Wedgwood knick-knacks, strode toward her and stopped just short of the settee.

He clasped her shoulders. "You said we never talked enough. So let's talk. Tell me."

Henri needed her to talk. To figure this out. Because

even now, even with the smudged makeup and tousled brown hair, she was damn beautiful. The heat of her skin beneath his hands was familiar and intoxicating.

He still wanted her. Cancer or no cancer. Kids or no kids. Though his hands stayed steady on her shoulders, he wanted to send them traveling on her body. To push her back on the bed.

Their bed—before she'd sent him to his own room after they'd returned from her surgery overseas. She'd said the surgery left her in too much pain to risk being bumped in the night. And somehow over time, she'd kept the separate rooms edict in place. He didn't know how so much time had slipped away, but day by day, he'd been so damn afraid he would say or do the wrong thing when she was in such a fragile state. He'd gone along with her request for space until the next thing he'd known their lawyer was drawing up papers.

He was done waiting around. He was a man of action.

After a moment of hesitation, she shrugged off his hands. "Talking now won't change us splitting up. You have to understand that."

"Then let's talk to give each other peace when we walk away." If he could keep her talking, they were still together. She wouldn't be closing the door in his face.

She chewed her bottom lip before releasing it slowly, then nodding. "Speak then."

He sat on the settee and held her hand, tugging gently. She held back for a moment before surrendering to sit beside him. He shuffled at the last instant so she landed on his lap.

"That's not playing fair."

"Then move."

Indecision shifted across her heart-shaped face, then a spark of something. Pure Fiona spunk. She wriggled once, causing a throbbing ache in his groin an instant before she settled.

He raised an eyebrow. "Now *that's* not playing fair."

"I thought you wanted to talk."

"I did. Now it's tough to think." He tapped her lips. "But I'm trying. We could start with you telling me what really made you cry."

She avoided his gaze as she said, "I had a long talk with your grandfather this evening. Seeing him fading away made me sad." Resting her head on Henri's chest, she took a ragged breath. Grandpa Leon and Fiona had always been close.

"I understand that feeling well. It's hard to watch, hard to think about. I miss him already." Pulling her closer, Henri softened as she wrapped her arms around him. Lifting a hand, he stroked her dark brown hair, releasing the braid that confined her curls. This was what he missed. Being close like this. Feeling her against him. "Are you really prepared to walk away from this family? My brothers, Adelaide…everyone?"

Fiona stayed against his chest, fingers twirling around the back of his neck. Shocks of electric energy tingled along his spine. His hand slid down the side of her body, gingerly touching the silky fabric of her dress, making him itch for more. The light smell of her perfume worked his nerves. It had grown silent between them. The only audible noise was the click-click-click of the ceiling fan.

"Perhaps they will still like me afterward." The words came out like a whisper.

"Of course they will." It was impossible not to like her.

"But I understand it could be awkward for everyone, especially for you when you move on." Again, she cut into his core.

"You already have me in a relationship with someone else? That's cold." He hadn't had eyes for anyone but her since they'd met. He'd been head over heels for her from the get-go.

"I imagine the women will be flocking to you the instant they hear you're free."

Fiona's face was close to his now. Her mouth inches from his. The breath from her words warmed his lips.

"But I only want you." He tilted his head, touched the bottom of her chin and kissed her fully, his tongue meeting and sweeping against hers.

The familiar texture of her lips, the taste of her, awakened a deep need in him. They knew each other's bodies and needs. He knew just where to stroke behind her ears to make her purr.

Fiona kissed him back, wrapping her arms around him, pulling him close against her. Her fingers slid into his hair, caressing along his scalp and grazing lower, her nails lightly trailing along his neck, then digging into his shoulders with need.

His hands roved down her back, the ridge of her zipper reminding him of earlier when he'd slid it up, link by link. Every time, touching her set him on fire. The silk of her dress was every bit as soft as her skin.

And he had once made it his personal mission to learn the terrain of every inch of that skin.

His fingers played down to her hips, digging in as he tugged her even closer on his lap. The curve of her ass pressed against the swelling ache of his erection, making him throb even harder. He nipped along her ear, then soothed the love bite with the tip of his tongue. Her head fell back and her lips parted with a breathy sigh that prompted his growl of approval in response. He kissed down her neck, to the sweet curve of her shoulder. His hand skimmed up her side—

And just as quickly as it had started, she pulled back, sliding off his lap and stumbling to her feet. Her hands shaky, she smoothed the lines in her dress.

What the hell? He struggled to pull his thoughts together but all the blood in his body was surging south hard and fast.

She stared at him, eyes full of confusion. "You need to go." Before he could speak, she made fast tracks to the door, holding it open even wider. "You *need* to go. I'll see you in the morning."

And even with the lack of blood to his brain, he knew. There was no arguing with his wife tonight.

Kicking at the cover, Fiona tossed in her king-size bed, trapped in the twilight hell between having a nightmare and being half-awake. The torture of knowing she should be able to grapple back to consciousness but unable to haul herself from the dream that felt all too real.

In the fog of her dream, Fiona pushed open the door of her childhood home, making her way across the kitchen and into the living room. Her father, a dignified-looking man with salt-and-pepper hair, sat on the overstuffed chair in the corner of the room, clutching the newspaper in his hand.

Something was wrong. She could hear it in the rattle of those papers clutched in his shaky grip. See it on his face when his gaze met hers over the top of the *New Orleans Times*.

"Dad?" The voice that puffed from her lips seemed distant. Younger.

He shook his head, his mouth tight as if holding back words was an ungodly tough effort. Panic filled her chest. She needed to find her mother.

Spinning away, she started roaming the halls of the three-story house, opening the doors. Searching for her mother. Chasing shadows that crooked their fingers, beckoning, then fading. Again and again.

At the last door, she was sure she would find her mother, a willowy woman, a society leader who stayed busy, so busy Fiona had attended boarding school during the week to be kept out of the way.

On her weekends at home, there just hadn't been enough hours to spend together. Her memories of her mom were few and far between.

Fiona opened that very last door, the one to the garden where her mother held the very best of parties. The doorknob slipped from her hand, the mahogany panel swinging wide and slamming against the wall so fast she had to jump back.

Petals swirled outside, pink from azaleas, purple from hydrangeas and white from larger magnolia blooms, all spiraling through the air so thickly they created a hurricane swirl she couldn't see through. Her mother must be beyond the storm.

Fiona pushed forward, into the whirlwind, flower petals beating at her body in silken slices that cut her skin. Left her with scars on her body and soul.

The deeper she pushed, the more the realization seeped in through those cuts. The painful truth sank in deep inside her. Her mother was gone. The cancerous hurricane had taken her mom, her grandmother, her aunt, leaving Fiona alone. The world rattled around her, the flap of petals, the crackle of newspapers, the roar of screaming denial.

Water dripped down her cheeks. Tears? Or rain? She didn't know. It didn't matter because it didn't change the ache of loss.

The garden shifted from her childhood home to the historic house she shared with Henri. Grandpa Leon sat in a wrought-iron chair, his fading memory darkening the storm clouds slowly into night. No matter how much time passed, she felt the pain of her shrinking family. The pain of so many losses. The loss of her unborn children. All of her failed attempts at stability and happiness paraded down the pathway. Losing her mother young, her aunt and grandmother, too, until there were no motherly figures left to steer her through her shaky marriage. Hopelessness pushed at her, wound her up as the darkness of the windswept garden became too oppressive. She catapulted herself forward, sitting upright in her bed.

It took a moment for Fiona to gain her bearings and to realize she was in New Orleans.

Sleep was anything but peaceful these days.

Taking a deep breath, she considered calling her father. They'd never been close and it had been a while since they'd spoken. But still, the nightmare had left her completely rattled. All of the pressures of her current situation were bubbling over.

She had to leave, sooner rather than later. She realized that even though she'd been protecting herself from the pain of having Henri stay with her out of pity, she was also protecting him from watching her fade away if the worst happened.

Her dad had never been the same after her mother died. The loss of her mother had shattered him. Though there was distance between Fiona and Henri, she still cared about him.

It was best to walk away. It was simpler to walk away than get more attached.

Morning runs had a way of clearing Henri's mind. And man, did he need some perspective after last night.

Sweat cooled on his neck as he pulled into his driveway, the muggy, verdant air mixing with the funk of his own need of a shower. He'd driven to the Hurricanes' workout facility and ran harder than he had in weeks. There was a renewed energy in his steps. Something that felt a bit like hope. Which was exactly why he was back at their restored Garden District house now. He'd been in such a rush to make it home before Fiona woke up that he hadn't even bothered with a shower. He'd simply discarded his sweaty clothes in favor of a clean T-shirt and basketball shorts.

Deep down, he knew he had to focus on the upcoming home game. It was huge for the team in a year that could net them a championship. But everything that was going on in his personal life was taking his head out of this season.

Henri shoved out of his car, waving at the security guards who were on duty. The two nondescript but well-trained men responded with a curt nod as he entered the old home through the back entrance.

As he turned the knob on the door, thoughts of Fiona filled his brain. There was something between them still. The kiss confirmed that. There had been passion on both ends of their kiss last night. Having her pressed against him felt so right. Natural. Normal. He needed to get her to see that they fit together. Bring her back to his bed, back to him.

Stepping into the kitchen, he found Fiona cooking, the scents of butter and caramel in the air. Her chocolate-brown hair was piled in a messy bun. Her sleep shorts hugged her curves, revving his interest. Glancing over her shoulder, she flashed him a small smile.

He wanted her now more than ever. But how to convince her that they needed to get back to what they had?

"You don't have to cook for me. I do want you for more than your body and awesome culinary skills." He eyed the Waterford crystal bowl of fresh blueberries next to her. An intriguing—undeniable—notion filled his mind, and he pressed himself against her as he reached for them. They'd always done best when they kept things light. That might well be the way to go with her today.

With slow deliberation, he popped a few blueberries into his mouth, eyebrows arching.

For a moment, she looked visibly riled. Damn, she was sexy.

Then she glanced away quickly and kept her focus on the task at hand. "I don't mind. I love to cook. At some point soon, I'm going to have to figure out what to do with my life."

"If you insist on going through with the divorce, you know I'll take care of you." It was all he wanted to do. To be the one to support her no matter what.

Setting a plate down on the island, she gestured for him to sit. He looked at her handiwork—a whole-wheat crepe filled with various fruits. A protein shake was already there, waiting for him.

"Eat your breakfast and stop talking before I pour cayenne pepper in your protein shake." She shook the spice at him before she carried over her own plate and the cut-crystal bowl of blueberries and sat down at the island.

Sunlight streamed into the room, filling the space with warmth.

"I'm a bad guy if I say I want to provide a generous alimony settlement?"

"I appreciate the offer. It's the verbiage about taking care of me that rubs the wrong way. Like I'm…"

"You're far from a child. Believe me, I get that." He scooped up another handful of berries, pitching one at a time into his mouth, the sweet juice bursting along his taste buds.

"I have a degree."

Henri nodded. "And you've sacrificed your career so we could travel together. I appreciate that. I thought you enjoyed our time on the road—"

She held up the cayenne.

He yanked his shake away, nudging her playfully with his shoulder. To win his way back into her bed, he needed to keep things light. "Changing the subject."

"Thank you." She set down the red pepper. "Enjoy your breakfast. I certainly intend to."

"As do I." He tapped the bowl of berries. "These are incredibly fresh."

"I haven't tried them yet." Fiona reached for the

berries, but Henri snatched them away, that devilish smile playing on his lips.

Nudging the bowl toward her, he stepped closer, closer still. He plucked up a particularly fat berry and fed it to her. Her lips nipped at his fingertips, sparking his awareness. And she seemed to be enjoying herself, as well.

"That kiss last night—"

She coughed as the food went down the wrong way. Once she cleared her throat, she asked half-jokingly, "Are you trying to choke me to death to avoid alimony?"

"That's not funny. At all."

"You're right. Bad joke born out of nerves." She looked down, her cheeks flushing with embarrassment. "Your breakfast deserves to be enjoyed."

"Thank you. We've had some incredible meals together, just us. I'm going to miss these times with you."

"You're accepting it's over?"

"You're making it tough not to." He eyed her over his fork. Frustrated. Determined. "Any chance we could have one more night together for old times' sake?"

"That's not going to happen."

He wished he understood why. The doctors had told him to give her space to process the shock of learning she carried the cancer gene, time to accept the long-term implications. They'd claimed that she would get over the self-consciousness, the grief over what she'd lost. But God, they'd spent so much of their marriage on a roller coaster of emotions. Trying for a baby. Miscarriages. Losing a baby in the second trimester. Then when the doctor pointed out how the fertility treatments could put her at risk with her maternal family's history of cancer.

Then her hysterectomy. Her double mastectomy.

So damn much to process.

He wished he had someone to talk to for understanding it from a female's perspective...but her mother and grandmother were gone, her aunt, too.

The realization dawned on him. There were women in his family. Strong, spunky women who could help him win Fiona back.

Because come hell or high water, he wasn't giving up.

Four

If Fiona had to be in the middle of a fund-raiser crisis, she'd at least found some peace that the crisis was unfolding in the sunroom of their restored Victorian home. The presence of the garden stilled her frantic heart, reminded her to breathe.

In a lot of ways, the sunroom had become her unofficial office. She came out here to think or to read old-fashioned paperback books from the library. She felt, in a manner of speaking, very turn of the century.

She let her eyes rove above the half wall, her gaze pushing past the intricate wrought iron on the windows to the garden proper. Lush trees and bushes nestled against a winding brick paver path. Taking a moment to appreciate the view, she reorganized her thoughts.

Sitting in an oversize wooden chair, she surveyed the table in front of her. It was a mess—iPads, laptops, cell phones and sticky notes littered the farm-house-style table. She was up against a deadline for the next fund-raiser to step in with emergency help for the children's oncology ward event since the other planner had had a heart attack. The concert hall she'd originally booked had backed out last minute due to a terrible fire. It hadn't seemed very likely that the hall would be fully operational again in time, so she'd made a few calls and switched the location.

Making this fund-raiser a success felt exceptionally personal. The proceeds from the event were going to cancer research. It was a cause she felt deeply about and she couldn't bear to see the children's event canceled or even postponed. Fiona did what she did best—she threw herself into her work.

Fiona watched how Adelaide worked on the iPad, intensely focused on the screen in front of her. She was logging a lot of hours on Fiona's project. It was even more impressive because Adelaide was in the process of launching her own sportswear line.

"You have such a full plate of your own. I don't know how to thank you for your help." Fiona was truly humbled by Adelaide's support, especially on the last two events. She'd stepped in, no questions asked.

"Being a part of the Reynaud family gives great opportunities to effect change. You know how poor I was growing up. The thought that I could improve other people's lives? I don't take that opportunity lightly. I just haven't figured out how I want to make my mark yet. So if you don't mind, I'll just hitch my philanthropic wagon to your star for now." Turning away from the half wall, she smiled warmly at Fiona.

"Then I'll gratefully accept the help."

"Well, I trust you can help me plan my wedding. You have the best eye for things, Fiona," Adelaide said, examining the way her engagement ring caught the sunlight, sparkling with the brilliance of the ocean on the sunniest of days.

Fiona put on her best face, schooling her features into happiness, though such a task took some effort. She could feel the edges of her composure wobble under the pressure.

"It is such a lovely ring, and you will be an even more beautiful bride." Tucking a loose strand of wavy hair behind her ear, she gave her future sister-in-law the biggest smile she could manage. "Truly beautiful."

The light reflected off Adelaide's ring paled in comparison to the emotion that lit her love-struck eyes and tugged pink into her cheeks.

Her future sister-in-law began to chatter. And Fiona would have listened on, equally joyful, if she didn't notice the text message that blipped across her screen.

It was a courtesy reminder of her upcoming doctor's appointment. They had results to give her and more tests to administer.

Suddenly, despite the bright, airy nature of the sunroom, she felt claustrophobic. Anxiety wrapped her in a grip she didn't know how to shake. An acute tingling sensation rippled through her arms, and the world felt farther away from her than it ever had before. Everything—her impending divorce, her uncertain health, the loss of family—crashed into her at once.

She recognized that Adelaide was still talking, but the words were lost on her.

Fiona must have looked as bad as she felt, because her future sister-in-law stopped talking.

Setting aside her iPad, Adelaide pensively tipped her head to the side. "Is something wrong?"

"Why would you ask that?" Fiona placed her cell phone facedown on the table. It was time to focus on tangible things, to push herself back into the present moment. Concentrating on Adelaide's concerned words, Fiona let herself notice the warmth of the phone and the coolness of the table.

"You just don't seem like yourself." Adelaide held up a hand. "Never mind. Forget I asked. It's none of my business."

Fiona decided what the hell. She should dive in and be honest—or at least partially open. And yes, maybe she was acting out of fear, because Henri's kiss had rocked her resolve to move on with her life. "It's no secret in the family that Henri and I have had trouble. We've struggled with infertility. There's more to it than that."

"I'm here if you want to talk." Adelaide walked closer to her, lowering her voice, her southern accent full of earnest concern.

"What happens if I'm not part of the family anymore? Your loyalties will be here, and I understand that."

"It's that bad? You're thinking about splitting up?" An edge of surprise hitched in Adelaide's voice.

It had been a giant mistake to say that much. The last thing Fiona wanted to do was burden anyone. It was suddenly clear that she wasn't ready to discuss this, not with Adelaide. Now she had to refocus, get them back on track. Ignore the pain in her chest and move forward. That's what she was best at, anyway.

Moving forward. Stacking a few papers into perfect order, she inhaled deeply, closed her eyes and spoke.

"Let's focus on the party. I need to get through the next couple of weeks and salvage this event for the fund-raising dollars—and for the children in the hospital looking forward to their party."

"If that's what you want." Adelaide didn't seem particularly convinced, but she also didn't press her further.

"This event is important to me. More so than the others." Scrolling through a web page, she gestured at the band options. "I need it to be perfect. This disease has taken so much from so many families." Not just other families. Her family. And now it threatened her, too. In a small voice, she added, "My mother died of cancer when I was young—my grandmother and aunt, too."

"I didn't know." Adelaide reached across to squeeze Fiona's hand. "Apparently there are a lot of things I didn't know and I'm so very sorry for your pain."

"Henri and I aren't ready for people to know about the divorce until the end of the season, when the papers will be ready to be filed, but I'm thinking now we aren't going to be able to wait that long. I imagine our secrets will be out in the public soon enough if the press gets wind of things."

"The lack of privacy is difficult."

"We've worked hard to keep things private."

"Perhaps too much so, from the sound of how little the family knows of what's going on. Family can be a support system." Adelaide patted her chest. "I consider myself part of your family."

"Thank you, but if we split…" She swallowed hard.

"Most of my family is gone. I only have my father left and, well, we're not close." Since all of her friends were tied to Henri's family and the football world, that left her facing a looming void.

"Fiona, I'm here for you if you need me, regardless."

"I envy your career and independence. I need to find that for myself."

"What would you like to do with your life?"

Fiona cheeks puffed out with the force of her sigh. "I'm an art major and I throw parties. If only I had an engineering degree to tack on to the end of that, I would be a hot commodity on the job market."

Before Adelaide had a chance to respond, Princess Erika stepped into the sunroom. She was Gervais's beautiful Nordic fiancée. Her pale blond hair was gathered over one shoulder, intricately woven into a thick fishtail braid.

"Sisters," she said, rubbing her hand along her pregnant stomach. Her announcement—and engagement—had caught the whole family by surprise since the couple hadn't known each other long. But their love was clear. "I rang the bell but you didn't hear me. The cleaning lady let me in on her way out. What are we doing here and can I help? I am at loose ends until after the wedding, when I begin school. And of course newborn twins will keep me busy. The calm before the hurricane."

The hurricane? Erika had a way of twisting idioms that was endearing. Fiona would miss that and so many other things about this family she'd grown close to during her marriage.

Adelaide shook her head. "Only you would think preparing for a wedding isn't enough to keep a person busy."

The princess shrugged elegantly, wearing her impending motherhood with ease. Fiona swallowed down an ache that never quite went away. She'd had such plans for her life as a wife and mother. She'd wanted a family, a big family, unlike her solitary upbringing. Maybe Henri's large family had been part of the allure, too.

Regardless, there would be no family for her. It hurt that this woman got pregnant with twins without even trying while Fiona couldn't bear a child no matter how hard every medical professional worked to bring about a different result. But that wasn't the fault of anyone in this room.

Fiona kept her gaze firmly off Erika's stomach and on her face. "Thank you for your offer of help. We would love to have you keep us company."

"Does that mean you will share your beignets?" Erika said with a twinkle in her blue eyes. "I cannot get enough of them."

The lump in Fiona's throat became unbearable. She loved these women…but it hurt. She knew it was selfish and small, but watching them get their fairy-tale endings just served as a reminder that she was far from having that. And Erika's pregnancy was so difficult for her to watch.

Tears burned as thoughts of lost dreams threatened her ability to hold it together. And she absolutely would not lose it in front of Henri's family. Her pride was about all she had left.

Henri's body ached from practice, but he still burned to talk to Fiona. So he did the sensible thing:

he went to the sunroom. Her operation station, as he liked to call it.

He turned the corner into the sunroom, only half surprised to see Adelaide and Erika working alongside Fiona. Adelaide, iPad in hand, pointed out something on the screen to Erika.

Everything was under control. A smile tugged at his lips. It felt good to see some bit of normalcy in the house.

Not until he saw the tears welling in Fiona's sherry-colored eyes did he realize there was something truly wrong. She was on the verge of falling apart.

In one swift motion, she grabbed her phone and opened the door to the garden. It rattled behind her as she walked into what she'd often called her land-scaped haven.

Every part of him screamed to life. He should follow her. Had to follow her. Feet moving of their own volition, he started toward the door.

But something stopped him. What would he even say to her?

It was time to call in reinforcements. With a heavy sigh, he sat in the chair by the table.

"Ladies, I need your help. Adelaide, can I count on you for some assistance?"

"The party is well in hand. Your wife is a master-ful organizer." Adelaide gestured to the scattered papers on the desk. Each stack was color coordinated with sticky notes.

Tapping his fingers on the desk, he looked up at her. "My wife and I are going through, a, uh, rough patch. I could use some ideas for bringing romance back to the marriage."

"I'm very sorry to hear that," she said with undeniable sympathy. But he could see she wasn't surprised.

How had she known? Had she sensed it? Or had Fiona said something?

Erika clasped her hands. "Of course we are willing to help however we can. You and Fiona are my family too now."

"Thank you. I mean that. I'm hoping you can offer some advice, ideas."

Adelaide eyed him curiously. "What kind of time frame are you looking at?"

"I need to move quickly. Fiona is…not happy." That was an understatement. If he could just find a direction to go in. Some clue.

Erika scrutinized him with a sharp look. "Should you be speaking with her about this?"

"Never mind." He shook his head and turned on his heels. "Forget I asked."

Erika called out, "Wait. I did not mean to chase you away. I am happy to share what I can, although I do not know her well. You want your marriage to work, yes?"

"I do."

Adelaide ticked off ideas as if she was running through one of her iPad checklists. "Help her remember that you appreciate her, that you still desire her. Don't assume she knows. And remind her of the reasons you got married in the first place."

He heard her and felt as though he'd already done as much. Of course he'd put Adelaide and Erika on the spot, since they didn't really know the depth of the problems. He was asking them to shoot in the dark. But he and Fiona had guarded their privacy so intensely and now he couldn't share without making her feel betrayed.

Maybe there was a way around it without telling them everything. He and Fiona needed to get back to the early days of their marriage. Back to fun and laughter. Yes, the romance he'd mentioned. Fiona had a point that they hadn't dated long.

They'd gotten married because they thought she was pregnant, and it turned out to be a false alarm. They'd both wanted kids so much they'd focused on that goal—until suddenly surviving surgeries became their whole life. "Let's just say we've fallen into a routine and this old married man needs some concrete dating ideas."

Erika leaned forward, expression wise and intense. "That is very dear of you."

Adelaide quirked an eyebrow. "And to think America's hottest athlete is asking me for dating advice."

He spread his hands. "I'm all ears."

And he was. Because the thought of returning his marriage to the early days, before life grew complicated, had never sounded more appealing.

On her hands and knees, Fiona rooted around the flower bed, decompressing after a restless night with little sleep. Henri had locked himself in his study last night after her future sisters-in-law left. God, the man was full of mixed signals.

She carefully separated the butterfly ginger plants from the aggressive weeds that threatened them. The butterfly ginger was a sweet plant, and the invasive species that shared the flower bed threatened to snuff them out completely. She'd made a habit of maintaining balance in the garden. It provided her a sense of peace.

Especially these days.

She was so fixated on the weeds in the flower bed she barely registered the sound of footsteps on the brick pavers. Casting a glance over her right shoulder, her gaze homed right on the muscled form of Henri approaching. His lips were in a thin line, strain wearing on his face as he went underneath the ivy-wrapped arbor, passing the golden wonder tree and the forsythia sage plants. He still looked like the man she fell in love with and married three years ago.

And that was what hurt the most. She was broken, in her heart, unable to let him or anyone get close. She didn't know how to push past the icy fear.

Henri said nothing. He simply knelt next to her and started helping her. As they sat in silence, the woody scent of him filled her head with memories, each more painful than the last. Of what they were in the beginning. Of when things were good. Of how terrible things were now.

"I think it's time we surrender to the inevitable." Her heart was pounding so hard and fast, she thought it would shake her to pieces.

"What are you talking about?" he asked, his voice raspy.

"Seriously? You have to know. But if you can't bring yourself to say it, I will. Our marriage is over."

Shaking his head, he said, "You're wrong."

"Why?"

"Excuse me?"

"Tell me why I'm wrong."

"Because we got married. We said till...um, forever." He yanked a weed out of the ground.

"You can't even say the word. *Death.* I'm not dying. You don't have to feel guilty over walking away."

Frustration crept into his features, hardening his face. He tossed a weed on the ground. "Dammit, that's not at all what I said."

"But I can hear it in your voice. You feel protective, and that's not enough for us to build a life together." She shook her head. He had to see what was going on.

"We got married because we loved each other."

"We got married because we thought I was pregnant and we were infatuated with great sex. It was a whirlwind romance. We didn't know each other well enough before trouble hit. We're not okay and we never will be."

"I'll go back to the marriage counselor. I'll listen. I wasn't ready then. I am now."

"Thank you, but no. I've had enough." She couldn't stay and have her heart continually fracture and break.

"Stay until the end of the season."

"What good would that do?" Leaning back on the ground, she stared at him.

"I can't file for divorce in the middle of the season. It may be simple for you to just call it quits, but I can't walk away that easily."

"Because of the bad press." It was a low blow, but she delivered it anyway.

"Because I'm not a machine and I can't risk the stress screwing with my concentration, especially not when we have a real shot at going all the way this year. You know how much I have riding on me. How rare it is for a team to have all the right parts assembled the way the Hurricanes do this year."

The request sent her reeling. "Seriously? I'm supposed to put off my life because you want to chase a championship ring?"

"Seriously. It's not just about me, Fiona. You know that. How many people look to me to lead these guys? How can I ruin their chances at being part of a once-in-a-lifetime team? Those opportunities don't come around twice. And there are endorsements to think about, commentator jobs. So many things ride on this season."

Since she traveled with the team, she'd organized family support for the wives and kids when the guys were on the road. She couldn't deny she felt a commitment to that community. Guilt stung over throwing this at him when she knew how much those guys looked up to him. While Henri was blessed on many levels with talent and wealth, many of the guys he played with definitely weren't. The running backs could well be out of football in two years, given the short life span of their careers. Some of the linemen had been raised by hardscrabble single mothers who gave up everything to help their kids succeed.

She would be putting the season at risk… Still, she couldn't stay with him indefinitely.

"When you retire from football, you don't have to work." That was the truth. The Reynaud wealth went far beyond football and Henri played for sport, not to put food on their table. He would have enough money to be just fine if he quit tomorrow.

"Yes, I do. I'm not the type to take on pet projects. I need a full-time job. That's who I am."

Pet projects? Is that how he saw her non-paying fund-raising? It sure felt like a dig at her.

"What's wrong with a life devoted to philanthropy?" She reached for straws, pushing him hard with both hands because he'd edged closer to the truth, the hurt beneath the facade, and she felt so damn vulnerable right now. She was hanging on by a string.

"That path is one you chose, but it's not the one for me."

Indignation blinded her. "Are you calling me a dilettante? Deliberately picking a fight?"

"No." His dark eyes were clear. Focused. "But I think you might be."

Her defenses crumbled and he saw right though her. Panicking, she didn't even know what to say as he brought all that masculine appeal her way.

"You're sexy when you're riled up." He stepped closer. "No matter what we've been through. No matter how many problems we've had or how much distance, know this. I want you in my bed every bit as much as I did the first time I saw you."

Five

Anticipation sent his awareness into overdrive. Henri needed to touch her, to wrap her in his arms.

She was sexy—a tangle of tousled hair and pure fire. And in this setting—in the middle of the garden in that little muted peach dress—she looked like one of those beautiful nymphs that classical artists were always capturing.

Every bit as alluring. And every bit as elusive, too.

But he'd gotten this close to her and he could sense the answering awareness in her, a heat she'd denied too often these last months. Now, extending a hand, he trailed it along the length of her lithe arm. Gentle pressure, the kind that used to drive her wild with anticipation. She turned to face him, leaning into his light touch.

Reaching her hand, he threaded his fingers through

hers, locking them together in that one small way. He was holding on to her. To them.

He pulled her closer. Mouths inches apart. Temptation and need mounting.

Her lips parted. For a moment, things felt normal. The air was charged with palpable passion.

And then it happened. She swayed back ever so slightly. Henri could see the desire flaming in her eyes even as he spotted the *no* already forming on her lips.

So he pulled back instead, releasing her fingers to tap her on the nose. "Lady, you do tempt me."

She flattened her hands on his chest, her fingers stroking, her amber gaze conflicted. "Passion between us has never been an issue. But it will only make things more difficult when we split for good."

He tried not to take that personally, forcing himself to focus on the action over at the tall Victorian bird condominium the landscaper had installed in the garden. Taking a deep breath, he tried to haul in some calm from the backyard his contractor had promised would be a haven for years to come.

"Why do you keep talking like we're over the border and a quickie divorce is already a done deal?"

Fiona's hands clenched in his shirt with intensity. "Why won't you accept that we might as well be? Why are you making this so hard? It's not like we've even uttered the word *love* in nearly a year."

He should just say the word if that's what it took. But for some reason he couldn't push it past his lips. He was saved from a response when a squabble broke out in the birdbath nearby.

Her smile was bittersweet while she watched the little wrens fly off to leave the bath to bigger birds. "You know I'm right. People get divorced even when there aren't big issues at hand. We've been through a lot with the infertility, miscarriages, my surgery, the stress of your high-profile job, as well. It's just too much."

Did she have a point? In some ways. But at least she spoke in tangibles now, delivering more straight talk than she'd given him in a damn long time.

And in a strange way she was making sense. They had been under an immense amount of stress. He hadn't even considered that his job added to the stress of all she'd been through. He had food for thought, and even though she was still attempting to push him away, he felt a bit closer to achieving his objective of reconnecting with her.

"Fiona, I hear what you're saying now, and I understand that—"

"Please, I'm not sure you do." She rested her hand on his. "I'm sorry, Henri. I need to move on with my life."

God, she was stubborn, and that turned him on, too. "You've made that clear. We're ending our marriage after the season—"

"After my next fund-raiser. *Or now.*"

"Okay, not arguing. In fact, I'm suggesting the total opposite. We agreed we need new lawyers. That will happen after your fund-raiser so we don't taint the event. We used to have fun together. Let's use this time to relax. The pressure is off. No expectations. No doctors."

She flinched.

He hesitated. Had he missed something? Before he could ask her, she seemed to relax again.

With a slow exhale, she took a few steps toward the

simple white swing that hung from a huge old live oak that spanned most of the yard. "All right. No pressure. Explain what you mean."

Seeing his chance, he needed to proceed carefully. Not push for too much.

"Let's just be friends." The closer he was to her, the more opportunities he would have to woo his way into her bed and into her heart, back to a place where they understood each other. Where their world would still make sense. "Like we used to be. People will ask fewer questions. We can take a deep breath."

She bit her lip as she trailed a hand over the wooden scrollwork on the seat back of the swing. "But some of the family knows there are problems and the rest of the family already seems to be guessing."

Henri shrugged. He didn't care what they thought. He needed to make it right with Fiona. That was the number one priority. "Then let them unguess for now. We'll deal with the rest later."

"Don't you want their support?" She stilled, a light breeze sifting through her dark hair and teasing it along one arm.

He remembered the days when he'd just sweep her off her feet and carry her to his bed when the mood struck—which was all the damn time with her. When was the last time they'd sprinted to the bedroom to peel each other's clothes off like that?

Shaking off thoughts that would only be counterproductive in his new approach, he picked a few daisies out of the rock garden for her instead, needing to keep his hands occupied with something that wasn't her.

"I want some peace for both of us right now, and something tells me you want that, too." He gathered one simple bloom after another, hoping maybe, just maybe, this peace could bring them back together. The fact that she was considering being friends spoke volumes.

"Why would you say that?" She stepped closer to him, watching him as he wound a too-long stem around the rest of the stems to hold the flowers together.

"We've been married for three years. Call it intuition." He passed her the bouquet, remembering she far preferred simple, garden-variety flowers to anything he could have found in their hothouse.

"I didn't know men believed in intuition." An all-too-rare smile—the ghost of one, anyway—lifted the corners of her mouth.

"I do. What do you say?" He gave her his best bad-boy smile. "Wanna go play?"

The cherry-red 1965 Mustang purred as they wound through the Garden District. The midday sun loomed large, warming the leather of the seats. In the vintage pony car, she felt more alive—more aware—than she had in years.

Fiona couldn't remember the last time they'd done something spontaneous like this. Or the last time they'd chosen the Mustang over the sparkly high-end automobiles at their disposal. She was happy with the choice, though. It blended into downtown seamlessly, attracting less attention and making them seem more like a regular couple.

For now, she could forget about the suspicious lump that might or might not be anything. She could forget about the biopsy scheduled for tomorrow.

And she absolutely would not allow herself to think of the worst-case scenario.

Today, she would play with her husband.

As the car passed through the streets, Fiona gazed out the window. Sometimes she forgot how truly beautiful this place was. Old Victorian homes lined the street, boasting bright hues of red and yellow. Wrought-iron gates encircled the majority of the homes.

What she loved most about New Orleans was the way the streets and sights felt like a continuous work of art. The cultures pressed against each other, yielding brilliant statues and buildings unique to this small corner of the world.

Pulling her thoughts away from the road to downtown, she cast a sidelong glance at Henri. His head bopped to some snappy song from the 1960s. He noticed her looking at him and he flashed a small smile.

He wore a plain T-shirt, cargo shorts and aviator glasses, his dark hair gleaming in the sun. Just looking at his beard-stubbled face made her cheeks sting as if he'd already kissed her in that raspy masculine way that brought her senses to life. Today he was rugged. Rough around the edges. Hot.

And a far cry from the normally polished quarterback the press couldn't get enough of.

As he turned the car down a narrow street, she couldn't help but notice the way the muscles in his arm bunched, pressing against the T-shirt.

Anticipation bubbled in her chest. The day reminded her of when they first met—from the impromptu backyard bouquet to the impulsive drive around town. "The suspense is making me crazy. What are we doing?"

Grabbing a baseball cap from the dashboard, he

gestured to the downtown district. "We're going to play tourist today."

Wind rushed over her, stealing her cares if only for a little while.

"But I've lived here all my life." She gave a half-hearted protest.

"And sometimes the more a person lives somewhere, the more that person misses seeing what's right under their nose. There's a guy on the team who used to live at the beach and he said he hardly ever hit the waves."

"Okay, I see your point. Let's go for it. Let's 'travel' to our home city."

"I thought you'd say that." He pulled into a parking spot and was out of the car before Fiona even had a chance to unbuckle her seat belt. He opened the door, extending his hand. She took it and a surge of desire seemed to ignite in her.

What was it about those easy words of his back in their garden that had given her permission to have fun today? Without worrying about mixed signals or holding strong to her defenses around him, she felt as though maybe she could relax again. Just for a little while.

Because when was the last time they had dated each other? It had been so long, so many months ago. Her heart raced as they made their way down Bourbon Street.

Trying to see the city as a tourist forced her to approach the street differently than she ever had. She began to notice the small details—the way the air seemed spicy, alive with the Creole seasonings of the various restaurants. As she concentrated on the smells, she started to notice what stores were garnering the most attention.

The street was bustling with people. Street musicians played with such artistry she felt moved by their passion. Her hand moved toward Henri's. Giving it a quick squeeze, she breathed in the moment.

Eyeing the carriages, Henri stopped walking. "How about we do this right? Horse-drawn carriage through the city. It's the best way to see this place, after all."

"I'd like that."

"Excellent. You pick the ride that will turn this town magical."

Henri gestured to the line of horses in front of them. Fiona studied a large bay draft horse in the middle of the pack. She liked the way he stood—tall and at attention.

"That one." Fiona pointed to the bay.

"Done." Henri went to talk to the driver, and they climbed into the carriage. There wasn't a lot of room, and Fiona found herself pressed against Henri. The simple touch of their legs against each other felt electric. She wanted him to take his hand and rub her leg. Her thoughts wandered over his body as she looked at him.

The jerkiness of the carriage caused them to fold into each other. Henri was wearing an older cologne— the one he'd worn when they went abroad a while ago.

Instantly, she was transported to the UK. It had been her favorite vacation.

"Remember when we went to Stonehenge?" Fiona peered up at him through her lashes.

"You were convinced you were going to travel back in time."

Nudging him with her arm, she laughed. "Those rocks hum."

"You've been listening to too much voodoo lore and vampire stories." He tapped her nose playfully.

Laying her hand on her chest, she poured a bit of theatrical flair into her voice. "I'm a native of New Orleans. You're a transplant. Give it time."

"Hey, I'm the New Orleans golden boy."

"Because you have a golden throwing arm. It's like you fast-tracked your way into being a native."

"Then good thing I have you around to make sure I stay authentic." He stretched his arm around her, the warmth of his touch pulling on her heart. She nestled into him, leaning into his embrace. Head on his shoulder, she was content to take in the scenery and keep pretending for now the real world wasn't ready to intrude with a biopsy needle in less than twenty-four hours.

So far, the no-pressure day was going far better than he could ever have hoped for. They were connecting. It was the first time in months that they'd been so open with each other.

So honest.

Shuffling a bag of tourist trinkets to one hand, he reached into his pocket for his leather wallet. Pulling out a few crisp bills for the vendor, he nodded at the woman's child as the imp put a handmade bead necklace into the bag. The fact that these mass-produced tourist trinkets were bringing Fiona and him closer together than the diamond jewelry he'd bought amused him.

The vendor was a rangy woman with too-bright red

lipstick, but she was friendly enough. She tossed a few chili peppers in the bag. The lagniappe. It was one of the things about New Orleans he'd liked since he was a boy on vacation—the gesture of the lagniappe always made New Orleans feel like a welcoming city. Which was why he'd felt drawn to this place when he was younger.

Henri scooped up the bag along with the others as they wound their way out of the store crowded with kitschy ghost memorabilia and wax figures of famous jazz musicians. "My grandparents used to bring us here on vacation when we were kids."

"You never mentioned that before. You always talked about the jet-setting vacations."

"My family's in the boating business, after all." That was putting it mildly, really, since they'd made their billions off shipping and the cruise industry. "Gramps combined business trips with a stop here, checking out the latest route."

"That sounds like fun." She ducked under his arm as he held the door for her, bringing the scent of her hair in tantalizingly close proximity to his nose.

"It's no secret my parents weren't overly involved in our lives, so my grandparents didn't have the luxury of just playing with us. My grandfather included us in work so he could see us. I like how you've worked in the same way for the team families." Fiona's capacity to include and integrate people was something he admired about her. No one ever felt left out if Fiona was involved. She had a knack for making people feel that they mattered.

"It makes sense. The ultimate educational experience for children is to travel along. Study the world as they see it. What did you like most about New Orleans as a kid?" She flicked her ropy ponytail over her shoulder as she continued to scan the streets, drinking in the sights while the heat of the day faded along with the sinking sun.

"The music. Street music." He smiled at the memory. "I would sing along. Jean-Pierre would dance. Damn, he was good. He's always been more nimble on his feet."

"What about Gervais?"

"He just quietly tapped his foot."

She snorted. "Figures. And Dempsey?"

"Those trips had stopped by the time he joined our family." Those days had been tough, integrating their half brother into the family fold. They were tight now, and Jean-Pierre was the one who'd left. Henri shook his head and focused on the moment. "Let's get something to eat. What are you in the mood for?"

"Someplace simple in keeping with our tourist day. Somewhere open air. And someplace where you will keep talking."

"Can do." He pointed to Le Chevalier. Ivy snaked around the outside of the trellis. It was casual and intimate—the perfect combination. "How about gumbo?"

Fiona clapped her hands together. "That sounds perfect."

Her French-manicured nails looked ever so chipped. Unusual for her. As though she'd chewed the edges. He shook off the thought and focused on the moment. On her.

Henri led them to a table in the corner of the outside patio. He pushed in her chair for her and then sat beside her.

Menus in hand, the blonde waitress bustled over to them.

"Are you enjoying New Orleans?" The lilt in her accent was particularly musical.

"Oh, yes. This trip has really made us fall in love with the city." Fiona played along, clearly enjoying the feeling of anonymity as much as he did. Since they were outside, he could keep on the baseball cap and sunglasses. His disguise was intact and his wife was engaged in actual conversation with him.

"Well, that's wonderful, loves. Take your time and let me know when you need something. I'll start you with some waters."

"We'll also go ahead and order gumbo." Henri smiled, handing the menus back to the waitress.

"Excellent choice," she said, writing the order onto the pad. And then the waitress turned on her heel and walked away.

"I love that we blend in here. That there aren't hordes of people vying for our attention." Fiona rummaged through the pile of bags from their purchases.

"See? What did I tell you? It's a no-pressure date day. It does wonders for the soul."

"Mmm." Fiona nodded, piling the trinkets onto the table. A little purple jester doll stared back at him.

He surveyed the stack of souvenirs. A masquerade mask brilliantly decorated in feathers. A T-shirt for him. A bamboo cutting board in the shape of Louisiana. A cartoonish, floppy toy alligator. The necklace with bright blue beads that would look lovely against Fiona's pale skin.

"Aha." She held out the voodoo doll. "Here it is. Best purchase of the day."

"You really are such a native," Henri teased.

"Hey, now. Watch out, mister. Or you'll be under my control." She wriggled the doll at him. Then she took its right arm and made the doll tap its own head.

In a gesture of good faith, Henri tapped his own head, mirroring the doll. She gave him a wicked grin.

"Your spunk amazes me." A rolling laugh escaped his lips.

Picking up the necklace, he watched how the sunlight caught in the blue beads. The glass was cut with the intention of splaying light.

"May I?"

"You may." Lifting her hair up in one hand, she turned her back to him.

His fingers ached to touch her. Sliding the necklace over her head, he worked at fastening the tiny clasp. He rested his fingertips on her neck, enjoying the softness of her skin. Breathing in the scent of her perfume, he leaned in, pressing his lips to her neck.

But instead of leaning into him, she recoiled away. She wrapped her arms around her chest and folded into herself.

He sat back in his chair, watching her, trying to understand. "Why don't you want me to touch you? It can't be the scars, because I've seen them and you know it doesn't matter to me." Couldn't she see that he wasn't bothered by any of that superficial nonsense? It was her that he cared about.

"That time we tried to have sex, you were different. It still is between us." Her voice was low, audibly conflicted.

"Of course it's different. You had major surgery."

"But you still touch me, treat me, talk to me like I'm going to break." She picked at her manicured nails absently.

"You're the strongest woman I know. You made an incredibly difficult decision and faced it with grace. I'm so damn proud of you it blows my mind."

"Thank you." She took a sip of her water, brushing off the compliment the way she always did.

He needed to make her see that it wasn't just talk.

"I speak the truth."

"I don't feel strong. I grew up pampered and spoiled by my father, who was afraid I would die like my mother. I don't mean to sound like a spoiled brat now—a kept woman who's whining because her husband wants to baby her." She chewed her thumbnail, then quickly twisted her hands in her lap.

"I fully understand you gave up a career so we could travel together, and you fill every other waking hour doing good for people when you could be like some sports wives and spend your days at a spa. Instead you're putting together six- and seven-figure fundraisers. You're organizing family adventures and educational activities for the children who travel to see their dads play."

"Why are you saying all of this?" Suspicion edged her voice.

A long sigh escaped from his lips. "To let you know I noticed all your hard work and your thoughtfulness. Your kindness. You're an inspiration."

"Then why can't you treat me like I'm strong? Why can't you trust me that I *am* strong?"

Trust?

He was caught up on that word, turning it over in his mind like a puzzle. Why was it that he could read the nuances of a complicated defense strategy, spotting the weaknesses and potential threats with uncanny accuracy, yet he couldn't begin to interpret this simple word from his wife? He lacked the right awareness for people, the right emotional frequency. He was grasping at straws.

This stumped him. He'd felt that he'd been protecting her, not treating her as though she was delicate crystal.

Damned if he knew the answer to her question.

Six

Opening the car door, Fiona swung her legs out, her feet hitting the garage floor with a tap. Before she could thrust herself up and out of the Mustang, Henri was in front of her, offering support.

Clasping his hand, she rose, their bodies closer than she would have guessed as she straightened fully. After the distance of the last months, it was as if her measurements of personal space were all off. Their breath seemed to mingle in the space between them. A faint flush warmed her cheeks and her stomach tumbled in anticipation—and nerves.

"I just need to put the cover on the car." Henri's voice was a dull murmur as he dropped her hand.

He strode to the corner of the garage and picked up a fabric drape for the vehicle, the cover crinkling in his hand. He always had a knack for keeping things safe and secure. The need to protect was part of his nature, and one of the things that was undeniably sexy about him.

The garage windows let the last rays of the evening sun pour into the space, bathing the walls in a twinkling amber light. She'd always loved this time of year—the way the autumn colors of the trees seemed impossibly brighter and sharper as New Orleans went from summer muggy to beautifully temperate. Even from her perch leaning against a sleek tool bench, she couldn't help but appreciate the way the wind whipped through the trees, gusting and causing them to rattle.

Fall was here. The time for dead weight to trickle from branches, even in the South, time for things to change. The hair on the back of her neck stood on end, goose bumps rippling down her body.

Her marriage was going to be one of those free-falling things. A beautiful leaf cascading from a tree. Perfect, vibrant—but not built to weather the harsh winter.

Holding herself together, she forced her eyes back inside the garage. Back to Henri as he tucked the car in for the night. His dark hair curled around his ears ever so slightly. He'd set aside the sunglasses and ball cap in the car on their drive home. Now, he stood before her in his plain, somewhat faded T-shirt. Perfectly casual. He wasn't America's poster boy or the team's golden boy. He was any man. He was hers.

And he was completely sexy.

Hitching herself up onto the tool bench, her leg swaying, she took in the way his muscled arms filled the sleeves of the T-shirt to capacity. But she also noticed the faint bruises that seemed darker on his tanned skin. The result of hours on the field, training with a resolve that had always made her proud. Henri's family had done well enough that he didn't have to work. And yet he poured his soul into his team.

As he stretched the cover on the Mustang, the car let out a low hiss. A tick of the vintage automobile.

Their date had turned quiet after their deep discussion at dinner. Had it been a good idea or bad? It was certainly the kind of subject matter their former marriage counselor would have encouraged.

In the brief time they'd attended therapy, they'd both alternated between quiet and boiling angry. Then they'd ended the appointments. She drummed her fingers against the cement tool bench, wondering if they had taken more time—tried a bit harder in therapy— would they be here right now?

Meanwhile, her looming biopsy had her stomach in a turmoil. She'd thought she had until the end of football season to ease out of her marriage, but the latest health scare put a whole new timetable on their relationship. If she didn't end things soon, Henri would absolutely dig his heels in for all the wrong reasons, staying by her side to help her battle for her health. Honorable, yes. But in no way related to love as a foundation for their relationship.

So this was possibly her last night to be on somewhat even footing with Henri. Their last night to be together.

Yes, she would have to get past the awkwardness of showing him her scars, but he'd helped her dress in the hospital more than once, seen the incisions. They'd even had that one failed attempt at lovemaking. He knew the extent, and certainly the scars had faded.

The plastic surgeon had reconstructed her body, and while he'd been the best of the best, the surgery had left her feeling less than normal.

But after the day she and Henri had shared, she found none of that mattered to her tonight. She'd married a sexy, generous, caring man and she'd never stopped wanting him. Spending the day together only reminded her how much.

This would be their last night to indulge in the passion she'd been fighting for months on end. She ached to reach out and touch him, to press herself against his tanned, toned body once more. To be with him. And after tomorrow…well, things might never be the same. So she'd put this on her terms. She'd go for this now and damn the future.

Fluffing her hair over her shoulder, Fiona inhaled a sharp breath, tasting the air. The scents of falling leaves and gasoline filled her nostrils. It was now or never.

"Henri, let's walk outside, savor the sunset."

He cocked his head to the side, his forehead creased with confusion. "Sure, sounds like a nice idea."

"We're blessed to have flowers longer in the season because of the greenhouse." And their garden was her own special haven, the place she felt most at peace. "Restoring that was the most thoughtful gift you ever gave me—other than those daisies."

They began outside. She took unsure steps, wending toward the greenhouse. Brilliant oranges and yellows flamed out on the horizon. A few birds trilled in the distance, chattering over something that sounded urgent.

"I'm glad to know there are happy memories for

you." His eyes wandered over their yard. Their home. The place they'd restored with a kind of passion she wished they could have applied toward restoring *them*.

She slid her hand in his, testing the waters for seduction. "There are many happy memories. I want to treasure those."

He squeezed her hand. "Me, too."

Henri's thumb ran gently across her knuckles. Slow and deliberate.

Opening the greenhouse door with one hand, Henri led them inside. The chill in the air was replaced by temperate warmth. The scents of rosemary and sweet flowers hung heavy in the air.

It was a stark contrast from outside. The plants in here hadn't succumbed to the change of fall yet. No leaves were hanging by threads; the flowers still bloomed. All was alive with possibility in this sheltered environment.

"Mmm. Do you remember the time we went to New York City?" Her voice was open and lithe as she allowed herself to look back through their entwined history.

"I haven't thought about that trip in forever. One of the best away games of my career."

"And?" she pressed. They continued into the greenhouse, heading for the back wall where there was a small clearing and some patio furniture.

"And also one of the best art galleries I've ever stepped foot in. Then again, having a built-in guide helps that."

He sat on the lounge chair, sinking into the plush cushion. Beckoning her, he patted the space next to him.

Folding herself onto the lounge beside him, she took a deep breath. "Well, my art degree is good for things like that."

"It certainly helps. It's probably why you are brilliant at assembling fund-raisers—you approach problems with such creativity." His voice trailed off as he stroked the back of her hair.

The simple touch sent ripples of pleasure along her skin, all the more potent for how long she'd denied herself those feelings. Those touches. She wanted to tip her head back to lean more heavily against him, to demand more. But after all the times she'd pulled away from him these last months, she wanted to be clear about what she wanted.

Spinning around on the lounge, she faced him. Scooting close to him, she slung her arms around his neck, drawing closer.

"Henri, I can't deny that I want you." She saw the answering heat flash in his dark eyes, but she forced herself to continue. "Please don't read anything more into this than there is, but right now, I just want us to finish this day together. To make another memory regardless of what tomorrow holds." She hoped he understood. That he wouldn't turn her away even though she wasn't sure she deserved him on those terms. "Say something. Anything."

"You've surprised the hell out of me. I'm not sure what to say other than yes." He stroked his fingers along her cheek. "Of course, yes."

Relief eased the tension inside her for all of a moment before another feeling took hold of her. His hands stroked up her arms. Over her shoulders. As the sun set, dim lights flickered on overhead via auto sensors. The warm glow added a romantic aura to the verdant space.

His fingers found the nape of her neck. Twisting her hair in his hands, he pulled her to him, their mouths barely touching. The feeling of warm shared breath caressed her lips.

Anticipation mounted in her chest. This moment was everything. She'd almost forgotten how fast he could turn her inside out with just a look. A touch.

And then his lips met hers, his mouth sure as he molded her to him. Tension and longing filled his kiss. It was in the way he held her. How he touched her. How he *knew* her. She melted into him, her body easing into his in a manner she hadn't allowed herself in forever. His tongue explored her mouth, making her rediscover a rhythm—a way of breathing. She dragged in air scented by hothouse flowers and Henri—his skin, his sweat, his aftershave, all of it intensified in the muggy greenhouse air.

Her hands sought his back, roving over the impossible cords of muscle as the passion between them picked up in intensity, as desire developed a course of its own. She wanted him more than ever. How could she not? This was a constant between them, burning hotter than ever.

Henri pulled back. The absence of his lips shocked her for a moment, and she blinked at him. Unsure.

A small, wicked smile played along his lips.

He held her hand, pulling her into him. His breath was hot against her ear. "Let's go inside, to the bedroom."

"Let's not. Let's stay here, together." She bunched

his shirt in her eager fingers, pulling it over his head as his grin widened.

"I always have appreciated your adventurous spirit."

His hand went beneath her dress. Nimble fingers teased up her leg, setting her desire into overdrive. He caressed a spot behind one knee, lingered along the curve of her hip as he kissed her, driving her crazy for more of him and his touch. She scooted closer on the lounger until she was almost in his lap, and he finally fingered the edge of her panties and slid his hand beneath the lace. Hunger for him coiled in her belly and she pressed herself to him harder. He pulled her lace panties down, discarding them on the floor.

Her whole body hummed with anticipation.

Taking a moment to appreciate his honed body, she edged back to run light fingers over the bruises on his arms. They were purple and dark, the result of sacks he'd taken and defensive players continually trying to chop the ball out of his sure hands. She carefully avoided putting a lot of pressure on them.

She looked at his bruises, suddenly aware of her own scars again. What would he think of them? She looked up to find him staring at her. Waiting.

"No spun glass. I am strong. A survivor." She needed to remind herself even as she wanted him to know it.

"I understand that. And before we go farther, I want you to know I do know what the scars look like now. More than just seeing you. After we talked to the doctor about surgery, I asked the plastic surgeon. I wanted to understand the during, the after, the years to come."

Frustration chilled her skin and the moment. "So

you wouldn't be shocked, turned off for life after seeing me in the hospital?"

He cradled her face in his hands. "I've never been turned off. Only concerned. I wanted to support you. And sure, I didn't want to look surprised or sad for you. I didn't want to risk hurting you, especially after what you'd gone through."

Some of the tension eased. She knew he meant it. And she refused to let some superficial insecurity steal this night from her. From both of them.

She turned her cheek into his palm and gently nipped his finger. "And now what do you think?"

She'd been afraid to ask before.

He skimmed his knuckles along her cheekbone. "That I'm glad you're safe. I pray every day you'll stay that way."

She clasped his wrist, stilling his hand. "Pity? Fear? Those are *not* turn-ons."

She needed to be clear on that point.

"Caring." He palmed her breasts. "It's about caring. You know me."

Delicious shivers of awareness tingled through her, her body wakening to life.

He eased off the rest of her clothes. Slowly and deliberately. With practiced hands, he unhooked her bra. The rays from the fading sun and dim interior lights danced against her bare skin, illuminating her completely. Scars and all.

Self-consciousness whispered through her no matter how much she told herself she knew the surgical lines had faded to a pale pink, barely visible. And her breasts were, if anything, perkier than before, although she had opted for a smaller cup size, going down from D to C. But he knew that already.

And she couldn't stop her thoughts from rambling.

As he took her in with his eyes, an unmistakable heat lit his gaze and a sigh of reverence passed his lips. He swiped a flower from a nearby pot. The stem snapped easily.

"You are so beautiful." He traced her scars with the petals of the flower, the timbre of his voice lowering an octave. The silky petals tingled against her skin, sparking desire in her bones. "Every inch of you."

"You don't have to say that." She deflected compliments so often.

"Have I ever been anything but truthful?"

"Not that I know of."

"Believe me then. Trust me. I look at you and I see beauty. Even more than that, I see strength, which is so damn mesmerizing it's the greatest turn-on imaginable."

A renewed commitment to this moment surged in her. Her hands snaked toward his bare chest. With gentle pressure, she pushed him back on the lounge chair. As the light from the sun faded behind the horizon, she surveyed the way his muscles expanded. He inhaled deeply. His eyes were fixed on hers, her need mirrored in his face.

Hooking a finger in his shorts, she edged them down and off. Climbing forward, she straddled him, pressing her hips into his. Feeling more alive than she had in months.

Henri didn't have a clue what had caused her change of heart, but after more than six months of being shut out by his wife, he wasn't passing up this opportunity to be with her. To taste and love every inch of her beautiful body.

Holding back from her every day had been hell. In the early days, of course, right after her surgery, it had been easy to give her space and time to heal. But after that, once she looked as strong and healthy as ever, he'd had to employ a ruthless amount of restraint to keep his distance.

And now, by some freaking miracle he didn't even understand, she was his again. Right here. In his arms.

He cradled her breasts in his hands, stroking, caressing, savoring the feel of her every bit as much as he enjoyed the sighs of pleasure puffing from between her lips. Everything about Fiona was sexy. Her wordless demands. Her hungry sighs. Her endlessly questing hands. He'd missed those touches. Hell, he'd missed the scent of her long, dark hair against his nose when they made love.

So now, it was sensory overload having her bare skin glide over his. She restlessly wriggled against him, the moist heat of her sex rubbing along his throbbing hard-on, driving him to the edge of frenzied need after so long without her.

He didn't see the scars, not in any way that mattered. He saw her. His strong beautiful wife, a survivor, who faced life head-on with bravery and strength. He thought of her giving heart, her philanthropy and the help she always gave to the other team wives.

What would it be like to travel with her again? To have her by his side in Arizona for his next game? Even though they couldn't travel on the same aircraft since he had to fly with the team and the spouses traveled separately, being with her, really being with her on the road, was something he'd missed. Having her in his bed at night was more than just a show of support. He missed talking to her, decompressing with her, telling her about the game he was passionate about.

He'd missed all of that as much as this. But this?

He felt as if he'd won the freaking lottery by taking her out on a date tonight. She braced her hands on his chest. He cradled her hips in his hands, lifting, supporting, guiding her...

Home.

The hot clamp of her body around him threatened to send him over the edge then. She felt so good.

So right.

Every glide was perfection as she rolled her hips and he lifted her up then back down again. Damn straight, sex between them was amazing. But he hadn't even remembered how incredible. Wasn't sure something this special could be captured in a memory.

Only experienced.

Their bodies kept time with each other. They pressed together, his mouth finding her lips. Her shoulder. Her hands twined in his hair. Her breath hitching, faster and faster, let him know she was close, so very close to her release. He knew her body well and intended to use that to bring her to a shattering orgasm while holding back his own for as long as possible. No way in hell was he going without her.

His hand slid toward her and he tucked two fingers against the tight bundle of nerves between her legs. Her husky moan gusted free, her head falling back. Her hair grazed her back as she rode him harder.

Damn straight, she wasn't a fragile flower. She took

him every bit as soundly as he took her. He reveled in the sight of her, her breasts rising and falling more quickly, her gasping breath, the flush spreading over her skin until...yes...a cry of bliss flew free from her mouth, echoing through the greenhouse. A bird fluttered in the rafters and, finally, he allowed himself his own release.

He thrust upward, deeply, his orgasm hammering through him. His heart slammed against his rib cage. The power of being with her was...more than he remembered. If he could even form words or a coherent thought. He could only feel each pulse of pleasure throb through him.

Her back arching, she fell forward against his chest. Her sigh puffed over his skin, perspiration sealing them together, connecting them further even as they stayed linked, his body in hers.

This moment had been what he was trying to construct for months. A moment of connection. Something real between them. Something built on emotion and trust.

Finally, after months of confusion and frustration, he felt alive with the possibility that this might be salvageable. Their trip to Arizona for his game would be like old times.

Lying in Henri's arms on the lounger, she planned what she wanted to do to his body through the night. Of course they would have to gather their clothes first, because running through the yard naked was out of the question. Even in the privacy of their garden beyond the greenhouse, there was always the risk of the media snapping a shot with a telephoto lens.

Nothing, nothing at all, could steal this evening from her. She had to make the most of this time with him, because this was likely all they might ever have. She couldn't even go to Arizona with him because of her biopsy.

If she even dared to tell him, it would only distract him from the game. Deep down, she knew he needed to stay focused. And she didn't intend to tell him regardless, though the excuse of work made her more comfortable in her decision to withhold information.

All of which she would deal with later.

His breath caressed the top of her head. "I've missed you."

"I've missed this, too. We've been through a lot, suffered lost dreams. Maybe if things had been easier for us…"

"I'm sorry, Fiona, so sorry I couldn't make this right for you. We can have children, adopt, foster—it doesn't matter to me."

As much as his words tempted her to throw caution to the wind and dive into the promise in his eyes, she couldn't escape the specter of fear that loomed inside her.

"It wouldn't be fair to bring them into a shaky marriage, anyway."

"You didn't say no to adoption outright, though. Not initially. Did you back out because you don't trust me? The marriage?"

"It was more than us. I wouldn't be honest if I didn't admit that my genetics have scared me lately. All the women in my family have died of breast cancer or ovarian cancer. As much as I worried about dying, the thought of a child losing her mother…" She swallowed hard. "That scares me to the point where I don't know what to think. So yes, adoption is something I've thought about. I wasn't sure how you felt."

"We really didn't talk about the important things in life, did we?"

As much as she wanted to share with him now, she couldn't bring herself to tell him about her biopsy tomorrow. She understood he would expect her to travel with him this weekend, to be there for him at his game. It was going to be hard as hell to push him away.

But for better or worse, she had to do this alone.

Seven

They made love in the greenhouse, the shower, again in their old bed.

Memories of their night together slammed into Fiona as she lay beside Henri in their four-poster bed. They'd spent the night entwined with each other. They'd slept naked. Well, he'd slept naked. Sleep had eluded her. She'd pressed up against him, too full of fluctuating emotions to actually drift off.

As morning crept closer, sleep was farther from her than ever. Instead, she watched the minutes tick by. Each successive change on the clock pulled at her heart.

She'd passed the night watching the steady rise and fall of Henri's chest as he slept. His rhythmic breath was raspy, his expression relaxed while she contemplated his bed-tossed dark hair.

She felt a pang in her heart. He was so damn sexy and last night would be the final night she would ever spend with him.

Even if the biopsy turned out all right, what about the next time? Fiona wanted to freeze this moment in her mind, to carry the essence of him with her for the rest of her life. The unraveling of their marriage was painful, and while a part of her loved Henri, she knew she was doing them both a favor by leaving.

So she did the only sensible thing she could. Fiona memorized him, noting all the small details that make a person complete. She watched the unsure morning light filter into the room. The muted sunshine seemed to get caught in his stubble, highlighting his square jaw. His long, thick lashes fluttered slightly.

Guilt and anxiety tickled her stomach. When he learned that she wasn't going with him, he would be devastated. The knowledge that last night hadn't changed anything between them would rock him to his core. She hadn't meant to rattle his focus before a game, knowing too well how hard that made things for him on the field. But there was nothing to do about it. Her mind was made up.

The sheets rustled and Henri shifted beside her. His even breaths hitched and he cleared his throat as he rolled closer to her. A growl of appreciation rumbled up from his throat an instant before his eyes opened to meet hers.

He slid a hand up to cup her neck and draw her to him. He sketched a tender kiss along her cheek, his bristly face scratchy and delicious. "Good morning, sunshine."

She pressed her face to his for an instant and allowed herself to savor every last sensation. "Good morning to you, too."

His arms extended out to either side. He stretched in a way that forced her to roll onto his chest. Ending the stretch, he wrapped his muscled arms around her naked body, pulling her close. A deep sigh filled the air as he cocked his head to the side to glance at the rising sun through the part in the curtains.

"God, it's later than I thought." He patted her bottom. "We gotta get moving. I have a plane to catch. I know yours is later, but wanna grab a quick bite of breakfast before I go? I know you have to pack—"

"Henri." She cut him short, unable to let him go on any longer. "I won't be flying with the other wives to Arizona."

He sat up slowly. "You're busy stepping in at the last minute to salvage the fund-raiser. I understand."

She wanted to use the excuse he'd handed her on a silver platter, but she could see now they'd let this play out too long. "Henri, last night was incredible—" she cupped his face "—a beautiful tribute to what we shared. But it was also goodbye."

Shock, then anger, marched across his face. "I don't know what's going on with you, Fiona, but you're wrong, dammit. Last night made me more certain than ever we are not finished."

She crossed her arms, pressing the sheet to her chest. "You can believe what you want, but my mind's made up. We can put off the official announcement to the public, however, we can't keep playing the charade at home and with our families. It's not fair."

Jaw tight, he studied her silently.

It hurt so much to see him hurt, and things would

only be worse if he guessed her secret. "Henri, you're going to miss your flight."

Exhaling hard, he turned away and flung aside the sheets, striding out of her room.

And out of her life.

The Hurricanes always traveled in their team jet, but today proved to be an exception. Their usual aircraft had been grounded for maintenance. Instead, the Hurricanes made their way to Arizona in a chartered luxury jet.

Henri wasn't having much luck enjoying the plush leather seats and open floor plan that made the jet feel less like a plane and more like a living room, the quarters as nice as anything his family owned. His thoughts stayed locked on Fiona. On last night and how damn close he'd been to winning her back. Yes, he'd made it into her bed again, but as always, one night wasn't enough.

Distracted as hell, he barely registered the interactions of his teammates. Freight Train Freddy tossed a football back and forth across the seats with Wild Card Wade. They hooted and hollered, pumping up the other guys with adrenaline. Even the veterans trying to play a card game in the corner were getting in on the action, fielding passes that came their way and taunting the guys on the other side of the jet.

Normally Henri would be leading the pregame amp-up charge. But today, he sat next to Gervais, the team owner, with a few of the other front-office members. Their seats up front kept them out of the fray.

Their Texas cousin Brant Reynaud, who also played for the Hurricanes, made his way from across the cabin. His yellow rose lapel pin glinted in the warm light of the cabin. He paused briefly to lean against the cognac leather chairs by Gervais and Henri, phone in hand.

"Did you see the Twitter feed? Our fans are loving us—all those pictures from the airport are viral." He gestured to his smartphone. "Someone on the media relations staff is doing a hell of a job connecting us to the public."

Brant clapped Gervais on the shoulder before continuing toward an empty chair by Freight Train Freddy, seamlessly reeling in a one-handed catch on his way.

The words barely registered with Henri. Pointedly fixing his gaze on the intricate chandelier in the center of the cabin, he wondered what the damages were going to be to replace the thing when someone hit it with a bad throw. Gervais pulled out his own phone to investigate the latest posts.

Gervais's face hardened as he thumbed through the Hurricanes' Twitter feed. A number of fans had rushed Henri and the other Hurricanes players in the airport. These types of things were normal. Fans always wanted autographs and photographs.

Today, however, had been a little different. Gervais's eyebrows skyrocketed as he flashed the six-inch screen of the smartphone to Henri.

Henri leaned over, hands resting on his thighs. Damn. The blonde from the airport who had gotten a little handsy with Henri had posted a photograph—one that had the potential for scandal. Not that it took much these days. People's marriages and careers had been ruined over less.

The thin blonde fan was dressed in high-waisted

shorts with a sheer chiffon crop top. She'd popped her leg and planted a kiss on Henri's cheek, anchoring herself by hooking their arms together. The image, out of context, didn't show the way Henri had tried to remove her and redirect her to a more appropriate pose.

A part of him longed for simpler, less connected days. Seeing how quickly the pictures in the airport circulated on Twitter left a sour taste in his mouth. This viral information was overwhelming, even when it was good news. When things looked slightly less than legit…viral information had a way of becoming deadly.

While Gervais was largely concerned with the team's image, he also no doubt worried about his brother. "Do you think that's safe, or even wise, given the current state of your marriage?"

Stomach plummeting, Henri ran his fingers through his thick, dark hair. "I wasn't encouraging her. I was working like hell to get away."

His brother nodded, but the stern expression didn't leave his mouth. "Oh, I know that. But you're in a career that puts you in the public eye. One picture. One sound bite. That's all it takes."

"And you think I don't realize that?"

Gervais didn't know the half of it.

"Just be careful, brother. Your marriage doesn't appear steady enough to weather this kind of pressure."

"What did Erika tell you?" In that moment, Henri regretted asking Erika and Adelaide for advice.

"No one has to. I know you." Turning the screen of his phone off, Gervais folded his arms over his chest.

"All marriages go through rough patches."

"Hmm." Gervais rubbed his chin in that wise big-brother way while saying absolutely nothing in the way of big-brother help.

"Don't pull that enigmatic bull with me."

Gervais gave a quick shrug of the shoulders. "You don't act the same around each other. You don't touch each other."

"You're in that newly-in-love stage, seeing hearts and stars." Henri tried not to snarl the words, but damn. Gervais's view of his marriage hit too close to home.

"You saw hearts and stars?" Honest surprise laced Gervais's voice as he unfurled his arms, leaning forward.

Henri jutted his chin in answer to that question. But the truth? He had seen stars. God, he'd been so in love with her then. What had happened? Or better yet, how had they gotten to this point?

"We're brothers, so I'm just going to say this and if it makes you mad, then I'm sorry. But here it is. We've seen with other couples in sports how infertility can put strains on even a rock-solid marriage," Gervais said softly. Sometimes he could be so matter-of-fact, peeling back the layers most people danced around.

Infertility clearly wasn't an issue with his brother, whose fiancée was already expecting twins after one weekend encounter. And Henri couldn't deny that stung. "I'm happy for you and Erika, but honestly, brother, do you think you're the one to talk to me about the strains of infertility on a marriage?"

"Point taken. Life isn't fair."

Bitter reality pulsed in Henri's veins as he shook his head. "Don't I know it?"

"Have the two of you talked about adoption?" Gervais didn't even turn when the chandelier finally took a hit, sending the glass medallions clanking together without breaking. He stayed focused on their conversation while Dempsey, the head coach, stood to call the group to order before the next pass broke the fixture.

"It's about more than not having kids. During a round of tests after another miscarriage, she found a lump in her breast." He'd carried the weight of those secrets long enough. And clearly, he hadn't been doing a good job of it, given how much Gervais had guessed.

"Damn. Didn't her mother and grandmother—" Gervais's voice had fallen an octave lower than normal.

Henri finished the sentence for him, nerves alight and fraying. "Die of cancer? Yes. She got tested for the gene and she's a carrier."

"I'm so damn sorry."

All the pressure and secrecy from the last few months came pouring out. Once uncorked, Henri found he couldn't contain the reality of his situation anymore. Fiona wouldn't be there in Arizona. Very soon, she wouldn't be part of his life at all. And that thought...it was too damn impossible to come to terms with. "We didn't just go to Europe for a vacation six months ago. Fiona had a double mastectomy and a hysterectomy while we were over there."

"God, Henri, I am so sorry. Why didn't you tell us?"

"She didn't want to."

Gervais gripped his shoulder and squeezed. "You didn't have to bear that burden alone. I would have been there with you."

"We didn't want to run the slightest risk of the press getting wind of this. Our privacy was—is—important." Still, it meant something to have his brother's support. He knew all of them would be there for him—and for Fiona, too, if she ever allowed anyone to get that close to her.

"Your call. Your decision. But I'm here if you need me, and there's nothing wrong with needing someone. You both lost your mothers young. That's difficult as hell." One thing about Gervais that no one could question was his fierce loyalty to his family. They were his tribe.

But that didn't negate the truth. A truth that still made Henri angry as hell. "Her mother died. Mine ran off because she was mad at Dad for not keeping his pants zipped."

"Death is tragic. Betrayal hurts like hell, too, like how our mom bailed on us even though her issue was with Dad's cheating. I can see how that would make it tough for you to trust. I've wrestled with that, too, in the past."

"Fiona isn't my mother." Not by a long shot.

"But she's leaving you." He paused, tapping the screen even though the image had faded to black. "Or maybe you've pushed her away?"

"That's crap," he quickly snapped. Too quickly? "I'm working my ass off to win her back."

"If you say so." Gervais looked away, reclining his seat.

"I thought you were here to help me," he couldn't help grousing.

Scrolling through his contact list on his smartphone, Gervais stopped at Erika's entry. He waved the phone at Henri. "For this mission, I'm calling in ground support from a certain extremely efficient princess I know and adore."

And just like that, Gervais asked Erika to deliver Fiona flowers from Henri.

Maybe he did need some more help winning back his wife after all.

The pain from her biopsy had nothing on the pain in her heart. The ache that was caused by a chapter of her life ending—the end of love.

She'd taken a taxi to the appointment because she didn't want to risk having the Reynaud chauffeur telling anyone else she'd been to the doctor.

Lying on the table during the procedure, she'd wished she had someone's hand to hold—Henri's hand. Not that they would have allowed anyone in with her anyway. Possibly having him in the lobby waiting could have brought comfort...but she'd made her decision and had to stick to it.

Now Fiona had sought sanctuary in the library, amid the books and art collection. She sat in an oversize Victorian chair, curled up in a throw blanket that featured famous first lines of novels in the design. She hoped the collective power of literature and art alone would seep into her veins and make her feel whole.

Settling into the chair, she had nearly become comfortable.

Until a knock at the front door sounded. Mustering energy and some bravado, Fiona made her way to the door, brown hair piled high on her head in a messy bun.

There were a lot of things Fiona was prepared for today. Company was not one of them. Her soul ached to be alone and to mourn her wounds and losses.

When she opened the door, Fiona's face fell. Erika was in front of her, armed with a card, a bouquet of lilies and baby's breath, and a decorative box of Belgian chocolate.

"Erika, what a surprise." Fiona forced a smile.

The Nordic princess braced her grip on the flowers and candy. "May I come in? Oh, and these are from your husband." She thrust the treats into Fiona's arms. "I won't be long. I have to catch the plane with the other wives."

"Of course, right this way," Fiona mumbled, urging her inside. She appreciated the gesture but somehow she knew full well this hadn't been Henri's idea. And it also meant their problems were becoming more public.

And she felt like a wretched ingrate. Forcing a smile, she thrust her face into the flowers and inhaled. "They smell lovely. Thank you."

Fiona set the crystal vase of lilies on the entryway table beside an antique clock. "Let's have a seat and you can help me eat the chocolates. How does that sound?"

Laughing softly, Erika patted her stomach. "The babies definitely need a taste of those chocolates. And they send their thanks to Aunt Fiona."

"Then let's dig in." Fiona led the way back down the hall to the library, taking comfort in the smell of old books and vintage art. This room was a place where everything was still in order—where things didn't have the pesky habit of uprooting and shaking her world.

Fiona tugged the red satin ribbon on the box of Belgian truffles. "Erika, you're glowing."

"Thank you. Double the babies, double the glow, I guess." She plucked a raspberry-filled truffle from the box with obvious relish. "Mostly, I just want to sleep double the time and eat double the food. Not very promising for a romantic honeymoon."

Erika's self-deprecation fell flat on Fiona.

"I'm sure Gervais understands." Fiona sat in a wing-back chair, cross-legged, the chocolates in her lap.

"He does. He has been incredibly patient." Erika looked around the library, absently rubbing her stomach as she chewed her candy. The motion played on the tendrils of Fiona's heartstrings. As if she could hear the pain in Fiona's heart, Erika looked up suddenly. A pale blush colored her cheeks. "I am sorry. I do not mean to babble on about myself."

"You don't have to hold back your joy." Fiona chewed her bottom lip, studying Erika's face. "Someone told you, didn't they, about Henri's and my fertility troubles?"

"I do not mean to pry." Erika dropped into a wing-back on the other side of the fireplace.

"You aren't. It's…well, I'm working on finding my comfort zone in discussing this with others in the family. It's painful, but that doesn't mean I can't celebrate your happiness. I love children and want to enjoy them." Fiona popped a creamy truffle into her mouth, but the high-quality chocolate tasted like dust. She set the box carefully on the end table beside her chair, leaving it open for her future sister-in-law.

"Want to?" Erika tilted her head, trying to understand what she was saying.

"I do. It's been a difficult road."

"Would you like someone to listen? We are family." Erika laid a strong hand of support on Fiona's forearm.

"We may not be family much longer."

Erika frowned and leaned forward to give Fiona's

hand a quick squeeze. The grace of royalty filled her expression. She spoke deliberately, a commanding reassurance filling her words. "I am so sorry to hear that. The offer to listen does not expire."

"Thank you." She reached to clasp her hand. "I hope you and Gervais are finding time to be together in spite of the busy season. That's important. Time slips by so quickly."

"I appreciate the advice." Erika inclined her head but—thank goodness—didn't call her hypocritical.

"And I appreciate that you didn't throw it back in my face, considering I have no children and am on the brink of divorce."

"You care about my future, Gervais's, the babies'. I can see that and appreciate it."

"I do. Henri and I rushed to the altar so quickly we didn't have much time to get to know each other."

"It is not too late to change that." Erika got up and straightened the books on the shelf, peering over her shoulder.

"How can you be so sure?"

"You are still here. So there is still hope, still time. Regrets are so very sad."

Regret. It was so damn hard to live with that hanging over her head.

Fertility was only half of the issue. And maybe, just maybe, she'd get the other half off her chest once and for all. The last thing she wanted was to live with regret, without ever giving her situation the dignity of a thorough examination. She'd already confided in Erika this much. Might as well see the situation all the way through.

"How are the wedding plans going?"

"Well, very well. We have a wonderful wedding coordinator."

"Is there anything I can do for you?"

"Just enjoy the day." She rubbed the swell of her stomach. "These two babies are growing so fast I may have to choose a new wedding gown."

"You will be a lovely bride."

Erika pointed to the couch at the end of the library. Taking a seat, she patted the space next to her, staring directly at Fiona. With kind eyes and a steady voice, Erika pressed on.

"You have something else on your mind. I can see that in your eyes. Since English is not my first language I tend to read eyes and emotions more clearly these days. Please speak freely."

"It's not my business, really." Fiona sat next to Erika, avoiding direct eye contact. Instead, her gaze fell on a Victorian-era depiction of the Greek goddess Artemis. Far easier to focus on art than the reality of her situation.

"Does it have to do with your difficulties with Henri?"

"I'm not even sure how to say this." A rush of dizziness pushed at Fiona's vision. Speaking this aloud would be one of the hardest things she'd ever done.

"Simply say it." Grasping her hand, Erika held on tightly, giving her reassurance and encouragement. Fiona couldn't meet her gaze.

But the words did tumble out of her mouth. "Henri and I got married quickly because we thought I was pregnant. I may have been and had an early miscarriage—or maybe Henri already told you this?"

Erika stayed diplomatically silent, just listening, which encouraged Fiona to pour her heart out.

God, how she needed to. "Since I had the one positive pregnancy test, I assumed…well…my point is, we rushed to the altar and didn't take the time to get to know each other. We have paid a deep price for that."

"I did not know the details. I am so sorry."

"Even if you go through with the marriage as scheduled, take time to be a couple. Your children are important, but having parents with a solid marriage will reassure them."

"Are you suggesting Gervais and I should not get married?"

"That's a personal decision. I'm simply sharing my experience and wanting to make sure you are certain. That's all. I hope I haven't offended you."

"Not at all. I insisted you tell me your thoughts and they are valid. My family pushes for marriage. You are the first to present the other side of the argument." She patted Fiona's wrist. "But please be assured. I have thought this through. I am in love with Gervais. I want to be his wife for the rest of my life."

"Then I am so very happy for you." And so very heartbroken for herself.

It was going to be a long weekend before the biopsy results came back, and either way she wasn't sure how she intended to handle things.

Eight

Fiona's whole body ached, even though only her left breast had been biopsied. While she'd put on a good show for her unexpected company the day before, she couldn't deny her relief at being able to suffer in bed away from prying eyes today. In the privacy of her bed, she felt the full force of the biopsy wash over her.

Erika had left with the other wives the night before, and Fiona had been alone. Over the course of the night, the pain had grown significantly worse. She'd hardly slept, finally dozing off at dawn.

Lying on her side, she kept the pressure off her chest. Although she was grateful to lick her wounds in private, her heart was heavy from needing to lie to everyone she loved. When Erika had stopped by, a small side of Fiona wanted to share the news of the biopsy with her. This burden was hard to shoulder alone, but Fiona knew there really wasn't an option. No doubt she'd distracted Erika enough from her impending wedding and giving birth to twins without saddling her with this, too.

Blinking back tears, Fiona wondered how long it would take for the pain medicine to kick in. Desperate for relief, she needed a distraction. Immediately. Glancing at the clock, she realized the Arizona game had already started. Had she really slept in that late, dozing off and on through naps?

Clicking on the remote, Fiona channel surfed until she arrived at the Hurricanes game.

Sitting up against the headboard in a sea of pillows, she situated the oversize nightshirt. One of Henri's shirts, actually, that still carried the scent of him. She'd allowed herself this small indulgence as she watched the game. Her fingers, seemingly of their own accord, fled to the loose cotton bra and bandage combination that shielded the places where she'd been pierced by the needle. Checking. Since she'd come home, the biopsy was a constant source of anxiety.

A long rumble sounded from the deepest point in her belly and she realized she hadn't really eaten anything. Easing carefully out of the bed, her bare feet hit the soft Persian rug, then the cooler wooden floorboards. She walked gingerly downstairs and riffled through the freezer—a woman deserved ice cream on a day like this. The best medicine a girl with an ailing body and a broken heart could get. She opted for a pint-size container of plain vanilla then plopped some of the chocolates Henri had given her on top. Taking a heaping spoonful, Fiona swallowed with bliss and made her way back upstairs to her bedroom to rest.

The flat screen mounted on the wall still echoed with the game. The daisies he'd given her earlier brightened the TV-lit room. Fiona had left the lilies he'd sent yesterday downstairs in the library in an attempt to spread out the reminders of what she was about to lose.

A heaviness pressed on her chest. This particular pain had nothing to do with the biopsy needles. It had everything to do with the large part of her that wished she'd gone to Arizona.

How she wished to be there cheering with the other wives, or even just waiting for him in the hotel room. To celebrate after the game. Her mind wandered back to the way her body had somehow, after all this time, synced to his two nights ago. Fiona wanted to have sex with him again, to pretend that none of this pain and suffering was real.

Scooping another large bite of ice cream into her mouth, Fiona turned her attention back to the game. Just in time to see the camera pan to the sell-out crowd, pausing on an older couple in matching football jerseys. The fans seated around them waved signs that read *Happy Sixtieth Anniversary!* and the smiling couple turned to one another to share a tender kiss on national television before the announcers moved on to comment about Arizona's offensive drive.

But her mind was stuck on that kiss. That celebration of a lifetime of love. Her mind rushed back to the gentle way Henri had cupped her head in his hands before kissing her. She tried to remember exactly the way his lips felt against hers—that gentle pressure of their kisses. The way his tongue had explored her mouth, leaving her breathless and ready for more.

And as she thought about him, the broadcast shifted to a close-up of her quarterback husband.

Soon-to-be ex-husband, she corrected herself. More ice cream.

Her gaze raked over him in his shoulder pads and away-game jersey, his features visible even behind the bars of his face mask. He was barking orders after the huddle, waving his arms toward the strong side of the field, reading the defense and making adjustments right up until the last minute in the way only he could.

He was one of the finest in the league and this season could be his best shot at finally earning the Super Bowl ring that he deserved to wear. She regretted not being a part of that. Even more, she would regret it if their breakup distracted him from that goal in a year when Dempsey and Gervais both agreed the Hurricanes had all the right pieces to win a championship.

But this was the business of breaking up. It was painful—the undoing of a person.

Suddenly wrought with grief—for her husband as much as for herself—her soul needed some reassurance. She reached for her cell phone and thumbed through the contacts, pulling up her father's new number in his retirement beach community in Florida.

One ring. Two rings. With each successive ring, she felt more uneasy about calling her father. What if he didn't answer?

She'd almost decided to hang up and abandon her idea to reach out to him. But on the fourth ring, as her heart pounded in her chest, she heard the phone pick up.

"Daddy?" She elbowed the pillow to nudge herself up higher on the bed.

"Fiona? Is something wrong?"

"Why does it have to be bad news for me to call my father?"

The lie slipped off her tongue. For a moment, she felt bad about being so damn practiced at lying about this terribly scary aspect of her life.

"Forgive me, let's start over. Hello, dear. How are you doing?"

Not well, and of course he was 100 percent on target that she'd only called because she was upset, but she had no intention of admitting that. "I just had some time on my hands and thought I would give you a call to catch up."

"Why aren't you at the Arizona game?"

Panic gripped her. She needed a reasonable excuse. Pushing the chocolate into the ice cream, she stumbled toward a feasible explanation. "I, um, have a cold, so it was better for me not to fly. Sinuses and all." Lame excuse. But better than the truth that would undoubtedly freak her father completely out.

"The game is a close one."

"You're watching? I don't mean to keep you."

"I can hear the game playing at your house, as well. Strange time for us to talk." His gravelly voice revealed nothing. Her father had always been tight-lipped. Well, at least since her mother had passed away.

"I'm sorry, Daddy. If you need to go…"

"No. Still plenty of time left in this quarter. I can watch this part on replay. So tell me. What's the reason for the call?"

Leave it to her practical accountant father to cut right to the point. Although that had made his meltdown over her mother's illness and passing all the more difficult to take. "Dad, what did we do for vacations before Mom got sick?"

"What makes you ask that?"

She was feeling her mortality? "Her birthday is near. I've been thinking about her more than normal. But the memories are starting to fade from when I was a kid."

The sigh coursed through the phone. "We'd take you to Disney. All you wanted to do was go there when you were small. Your mom would plan the whole trip—character breakfasts and character lunches. She loved Disney because it made you glow from the inside. Your mom would always take a bag of glitter with us and she'd sprinkle it on you before we'd walk through the main gates. Called it pixie dust and told you if you believed enough, your dreams would come true."

"I barely remember that." A sad smile played on her lips as she gripped the phone with a renewed intensity.

"Fiona? I'm not good about remembering to phone, but I'm glad to hear your voice. I'll miss your mother for the rest of my life. It was nice to enjoy that memory with you."

Sometimes, Fiona was struck at the way the memory of her mother elicited so much emotion from her father. He was normally so stoic, so practical. It always caught her off guard when he fell into telling stories about his bride, who'd been called back to heaven far too young.

Fiona hung up the phone not feeling any more assured about her life. Her heart swelled with the knowledge of too many deaths and too many people who had to deal with the memory of loved ones claimed by cancer.

Rather than feeling comforted, Fiona felt a new kind of sadness settle into her veins. Hearing the strain in her dad's voice as he recalled his late wife affirmed the logical reason that she had to leave Henri. If she left now, he wouldn't be hurt the way her dad was.

But that also meant she had to face this alone. Selfishly, that scared her to her core.

Henri had a lot of reasons to feel out of sorts. The Arizona game hadn't panned out for a few reasons. Though the one that continued to be the real source of agitation was the fact that Fiona had been states away from him.

Grabbing his duffel bag, Henri left the chauffeured car and headed through the front gates and up the walkway toward their Garden District home. The old three-story Victorian loomed ahead of him, jutting against the storm clouds brewing in the background.

Clicking open the door, he was greeted by silence.

Setting his keys down on the kitchen counter, he noticed the lilies he'd sent were in the middle of the kitchen island, card askew next to the vase.

While he had no idea what he was walking into, he was certain that he had to see Fiona. The need to be there for her—no matter how hard she pushed against the idea—gave him purpose.

He took the minimal amount of texting between them as a good sign. Though they didn't talk on the phone, they had still communicated. For Henri, as long as a line of communication was still open, he harbored hope for them. Believed they could work this out.

To allow his mind to wander to the alternative was

absolutely not an option. It admitted defeat, made him a quitter. And Henri was not about to do that when it came to his wife.

Quietly, he made his way up the stairs to her room, hoping to find her lost in a good book.

Instead, when he gingerly nudged the door open, he saw she was asleep. Out cold, really.

Something about her sleeping form seemed off. She was paler than normal, wearing a loose night-shirt and couched by pillows on both sides. Her bare leg was thrown over one of the pillows, which made his thoughts wander back to their night together. How damn amazing it had been to be back in bed with her again. It had been even better than before, because now there was no way in hell he would ever take for granted the gift of being with her.

Inside her.

Except then his mind hitched on the fact that something was off in her position, the way she lay with all those pillows. Her inexplicable paleness struck him as deeply odd. It registered in his brain, but he didn't know what to do with the information. So he tucked it away, saved it for later. He was too tired to analyze that now.

Unable to pull himself away from her, he slumped into the fat wing-back chair by the fireplace. The cushions were comfortable and he relaxed. His eyes grew heavy, until he was barely able to keep his lids open. And then they closed completely, and he drifted off.

His dream took him to a memory of when they'd just met. He'd whisked her away to watch him play a game in Philadelphia. The Hurricanes had had their

first major win, and all he'd wanted to do was celebrate with her.

In the hotel room postgame, the passion that had
danced between them was a palpable energy.

"How about a double victory?" she'd breathed coyly
into his ear, hands traveling slowly down his chest and
stopping at his waistband. Her hair had been longer
then, wilder. There'd been an unquenchable desire in
her eyes, and he'd wanted to do his damnedest to give
her everything, all of him. They were young—lives
and potential sparking before them.

The next day, they'd made themselves at home in
Philadelphia, ducking in and out of museums and art
galleries. While most people assumed Henri was in-
capable of appreciating culture due to his occupation,
Fiona had simply rolled with his interest. Being an art
major, she could have easily made him feel inferior or
assumed that he was showboating.

But Fiona would never do something like that. The
appreciation of art, she'd always said, didn't take a
degree—it took appreciation for the human soul. And
so, they'd stolen hours in that city, getting to know
each other, body and soul.

On that trip, he'd known there was something that
bound them together, a passion that twined them together. Yes, there was an undeniable physical compo-
nent, but that was only half of it.

They'd returned to the hotel after debating the
meanings of paintings and other fine points of culture. Back in the hotel, he'd begun to learn the way she
liked to be touched, exploring the fire that burned beneath her skin. He needed to capture her as she was in
this moment. And so, in the dream, he began to brush

paint over her, to make her immortal on canvas. And what a muse she was for a man who'd never even considered himself an artist.

But then the dream shifted, as they often did. Fiona's surety and fire had been dulled, replaced by a self-consciousness he understood but couldn't fix.

He watched her fade in his arms, become ashen. The paint he'd used to capture her beautiful lines and curves ebbed away. In their stead, her body on the canvas was covered in scars.

Sweat pooled on his brow and he woke up with a start. Eyes adjusting to reality, he came to terms with the fact that he was dreaming.

He stayed in the chair because if he moved closer he wouldn't be able to resist touching her, making the dream a reality.

Casting a glance at Fiona, he was relieved to see her there. In the moment between sleep and alertness, he'd been afraid that she might be gone, fading away even now.

She tossed to her side, facing him now. His eyes roved over her, and he wanted to reach out and hold her. There had to be something—anything—he could do to win her back. So she missed a game. In the grand scheme of things, that didn't have to make or break this.

Maybe he'd take her to the new exhibit at the art gallery.

His thoughts on the gallery were short-lived. As he studied her, he noticed something dark against the white nightshirt.

Something that looked an awful lot like blood.

* * *

Fiona found it hard to stay asleep. The pain medicine had worn off, making it impossible to find a comfortable position.

Eyes fluttering open, she blinked into focus. Out of the corner of her eyes, she noticed a man in the wing-back chair. Momentary panic flooded her mind until she was fully awake.

Henri. He was back and in their room, his face stoic and hard.

Very slowly, she sat up. Pain pulsated. Fiona did her best to hide the wince that tore through her.

"Welcome back. Congratulations on a good game."

"We lost," he said briefly, curtly.

She understood how upset he could be over a loss. She leaned back against the pillows. The pain meds had her so woozy she wasn't sure she trusted herself to walk. "Defense wasn't at their best. You can only do so much. You threw two touchdown passes and ran another. But then you don't need me to recap what happened. I'm sorry."

"Are you?" Crossing his arms, anger throbbed in his voice.

"What do you mean?" She sat against the pillows, breathing through the pain that rocked her body.

"Are you sorry?"

"Of course I'm disappointed for you. I know how much a win means to you. Just because I knew the time had come for me to stop attending, that doesn't mean I won't be following the team's progress."

"Sure." His voice was sullen and she noticed, in the half light from the lamp by the wing-back chair, that his lips had thinned into a hard line.

"Henri? What's with the clipped answers?" She was too foggy from pain meds that weren't doing enough to dull the ache to sort through these mixed signals from him. "I understand you're unhappy with my decision to not attend the game—"

"I'm not happy with your decision to keep me in the dark about the real reason you stayed in New Orleans."

How had he found out? She followed the line of his gaze and realized he was looking directly at her left breast where...

Oh, God. Her biopsy incision was leaking spots of blood.

Nine

A jumble of emotions played bumper cars in Henri's mind. The blood on her left breast…the way she tried so hard to push him away.

How could she keep this from him? Frustration—and, hell yes, fear—seized his jaw. He ground his teeth, feeling something that felt a bit like betrayal.

That she had kept him from knowing something major—and potentially life threatening—was too much to digest.

His fingers pressed into the arms of the chair as he tried stabilizing himself. Part of him wanted to run over to her side, to hold her tight against him. But knowing she was sick and in recovery, the possibility and fear of injuring her made him stay firmly planted in his chair.

Scared as hell.

"What's going on?"

"I think you've already guessed." She tugged at the white covers on the bed. But she didn't look directly at him.

A lump grew in his throat. Terrible possibilities ran through his mind. "Were you even going to tell me at all?"

She tipped her chin upward. "Not if I didn't have to. No need for both of us to worry."

They'd fallen so far apart that they didn't share something as huge as this? He'd been by her side every step of the way through medical treatments, and now she was trying to cut him out of her life. Completely. Excise him like cancer.

No. Not a chance. "Details," he demanded softly, but firmly. "I want details. We're still married. We owe each other that much."

"It's just a biopsy of a lump that's likely fatty tissue dissolving. The oncologist is almost certain it's nothing to be concerned about."

She said it as casually as someone reporting the weather. He felt the distance spread between them like an ever-collapsing sinkhole.

Oncologist? But no, it wasn't serious. "If it was nothing, you would have told me. This is why you didn't go to the game. I would have understood."

She pushed her tousled hair back, her eyes fuzzy with what appeared to be the effects of pain meds— and sure enough, a bottle rested on her bedside table. "You would have been distracted. You would have gone crazy worrying. Look at how you're reacting now."

"I am in control. Here for you, always." Why couldn't she see that?

"That's good and honorable of you to say, but it's not the reason I want you staying with me."

"So if I hadn't seen the spots of blood you wouldn't have told me at all?"

Drawing a pillow in front of her chest, she let out a small sigh. "If the worst happens, then of course you would find out. Otherwise there was no reason to upset you."

The way she discussed her health with such nonchalance rubbed him raw. As if the only reason he would care to know if she was sick was bound up in some sense of honor and duty. That did him a disservice, minimized their bond. He did not stay with her merely for appearances' sake or to come across as honorable. Dammit, why couldn't she see that?

"Did it occur to you I would want to know, to be there to support you?"

"Thank you. But you don't have to do that anymore." She smoothed a wrinkle on the pillow and gave him a pointed stare.

"I'm your husband, dammit." He reined in his temper. "I'm sorry. I didn't mean to snap at you. Could I get you something to drink? Or an ice pack for the biopsy site?"

"You know the drill." She slumped back on the pillows, her eyes sad.

"I do. Is that so wrong?"

"I don't want you feeling sorry for me."

He ignored that. Couldn't even imagine how to make her understand his desire to care for her had nothing to do with pity.

"When will you hear from the doctor?"

"Next week."

"I have one question. How long have you known?"

"Since the day of the pet rescue fund-raiser."

He inhaled sharply. He pressed his fist to his mouth—he'd hoped she had only recently found out, that it had been some sort of emergency operation. That would be much easier to swallow.

"You weren't late because your car broke down. You've been lying all week."

"I've been protecting you and protecting my privacy."

The bedroom started to become suffocating as he looked around, seeing the life they had jointly built. It all felt like a lie. Some kind of story he'd been telling himself.

More frustration piled on top of the old, building up inside him when he was already exhausted and on edge. He knew somewhere in his gut that getting out of this room was his only option. Before he said something he'd regret.

"Right." Shoving the chair out from underneath him, he sprung to his feet. From the threshold, he called over his shoulder, "I'll get you that ice pack."

With every step, Fiona drew in sharp breaths. The movement pounded in her chest, causing pain to spiderweb through her shoulder.

Of all the ways she'd envisioned Henri finding out about the biopsy, this hadn't been one of them. With slow, determined steps, she made it to the first-floor landing and caught a glimpse of her reflection in the hallway mirror.

The mirror was expansive—and Victorian. Cherubs with lutes and lyres danced down the frame, twisting and turning in endless patterns. She'd found it at a flea market years ago and fallen in love with the distressed glass.

As she examined her reflection, depression edged her vision. She was a mess. Tempest tossed. Those were her initial assessments.

Her brown hair was swept up in a high ponytail but was completely disrupted from troubled sleep. All her tossing and turning had loosened it. Her pallid complexion and tired eyes did nothing to improve matters. Pulling on the corner of her clean oversize shirt, she felt like a shadow.

Clutching her favorite Wedgwood bowl full of ice cream, she charged into the kitchen. When she rounded the corner, a wave of nausea overcame her. A by-product of the pain medicine. Taking a moment to regain her balance and calm her stomach, she eyed Henri nervously.

He was leaning against the kitchen island with his back to her. He fumbled with the ice pack, but his head was cocked to the side, examining the news story on television.

It was entertainment news, overhyped coverage of celebrity outings and gossip.

Spinning into focus was a photograph of Henri with another woman. Her body was pressed against his.

Old news. That had already popped up on Fiona's radar. She knew such a photograph didn't mean a damn thing. Fans were sometimes aggressive and pushy. Henri might be a lot of things, but a cheater? Not in his wheelhouse.

Still, sadness swept over her as her toes curled against the cool tile floor.

This photograph might not be real…but after their divorce was finalized? Well, then these types of photographs might actually be evidence of a new relationship for Henri. Her heart fell ten stories in her chest as she stared at him.

Bad enough to end a marriage and know that your ex would probably move on and find someone new. That dynamic would be much more intense for her. Henri, rising star quarterback, would be front and center in the news. She'd be forced to watch him fall in love with someone else.

The thought hit her like a ton of bricks.

He must've felt her eyes on him. He whirled around, face flushed, pointing at the screen. "That's not what—"

"I know it isn't." She steadied herself on the coffee bar.

"You do? You trust me even now?"

"I trust that you wouldn't sleep with another woman while you're still married to me." Knowing that made it all the tougher to walk away from this man. He was a good person. He deserved better from life than he'd gotten in their marriage. She knew she wasn't easy to live with and her ability to deal with stress—well, here they were.

"Thank you for trusting me." Some of the stiff tension in his shoulders eased, although she didn't think for a moment he'd forgiven her for holding back.

"I believe in your honor, your sense of fair play." That had never been a question.

"I've never wanted a woman as much as I want you, always."

Her hands wrapped her body in a protective cocoon. Tears pushed at the edge of her vision. "But I'm not the woman you married."

He stepped toward her and wrapped his hands around her waist. Pulling her into him, he whispered into her hair, breath hot on her ear, "You're every bit as beautiful. No matter what else happens between us, the attraction hasn't stopped."

"Even with the surgeries?" The words squeaked out, finding vulnerable life in the small space between them.

"I still see you." He lowered his face to hers.

Fiona wanted to believe him. Wanted things to just stop spinning out of control. But...but there was physical evidence that she could never be the same.

"But there are scars. Even with the best plastic surgeon money could buy. And there's always going to be the specter of another lump and biopsy."

"I married you for what's inside. And I'd like to think that's what you wanted me for, too." He stroked her back with warm, strong hands. "Even if there had been no reconstruction at all, I would want you. You know that."

"I do. And it makes it all the tougher to resist you."

"Then don't resist me." Tipping up her chin, he gently pressed his lips to hers.

For the briefest moment, she indulged herself in the kiss. Let herself melt into his lips and the beautiful familiarity of being in his arms, of letting the musky scent of him fill her senses. After the fear and stress of the past day, she took comfort from his strong arms and the hard wall of his chest. The steady beat of his heart was echoed by hers; they were in sync. They'd been that way once, so in tune with each other. God, she hadn't imagined all of it, had she?

She deepened the kiss, loving the taste of him and the hint of toothpaste. She gripped his T-shirt in tight fists as she nipped his bottom lip. Henri's hands fell gently to her shoulders.

"Careful, Fiona," he whispered, brushing his lips along her mouth, then her cheek.

It was a tender, lovely moment...and yet there was something off. In the way he held her, maybe? His touch was far too light.

She angled back to study his brown eyes awash with molten emotions. "Henri? What's going on? This feels suspiciously like you're treating me as if I'm some fragile glass figurine. Like spun glass. Like when I got the operations six months ago."

His eyes went so dark the ache was downright tangible. "Damn straight I'm being careful with you. You're bleeding, on pain meds, and I wasn't there with you. How the hell else am I supposed to treat you?"

His pain reached out to her until she could barely breathe from the weight of it. Images filled her mind of her father, frozen in his reading chair, newspaper upside down in his tight-fisted grip as tears streaked down his face. Her grandmother and aunt shushing her, guiding her from the room. Later helping her pack for boarding school. Then college. Then they were gone, too. The women's husbands had all stood like hollow shells at their funerals.

Oh, God, it was too much. She needed space. Air. More space. She couldn't think clearly. She was about to shatter like the glass he seemed to think she was made of. And of course he would pick up the pieces no matter how those shards stabbed at him.

Breaking contact, she laid a hand on his chest. "I think you should stay at your family's place tonight."

Lips thinning into a stoic mask, he took a deep breath. His jaw grew taut. But his emotions stayed hidden. She'd seen him do that often in the past, protect her from anything unpleasant—or anything real.

Stepping away from her, he folded his arms over his chest. "We're not divorced. And I'm not leaving you here alone when you're recovering."

She also knew that look well. An entire line from an opposing team wouldn't stand a chance of sacking the immovable force he'd become.

Fiona filled her morning with forced movement. She needed to stay busy, to bounce back from the biopsy and from the impending fracturing of her heart.

Henri had left for the gym early in the morning. She'd been awake when she heard him make his way down the stairs. Part of her wanted to crawl out of bed to talk to him. Fiona knew better, though. She had to guard her heart. He'd only briefly come to the doorway and told her he wasn't comfortable with her being alone on pain meds, so he'd arranged cleaning help for the day and a car to drive her if she wished to go anywhere.

The stony look on his face didn't leave room for argument. And he was right. She needed help and should be grateful. In her need to protect him from hurt she was still causing him pain, and she couldn't seem to work her way out of the messy maze she'd made of her life.

So she'd stayed in bed waiting until she heard his car drive away before she got up and dressed herself.

Pulling her thoughts back to the present, she tried to focus on the sensation of sun on skin. She and the other Reynaud women were lounging by the oversize pool at the main family complex on Lake Pontchartrain. Giggles surged through the air—the family was at peace. Several team wives were there as well, getting to know Erika better, which was part of the reason Fiona had felt she needed to be here. Hell, she wanted to be here.

But it was tougher than she expected, watching them joke with each other, all so happy and healthy.

All of them except for her.

Though fall was settling in, the heated pool provided sanctuary from the light, chilly breeze. Fiona watched the sunlight dance in the pool as Erika dipped a toe, testing the water.

Fiona sighed, listening to the chatter of bugs and birds as she tried to appear normal. Such a difficult ruse, especially since she'd had no choice but to make use of the chauffeur if she'd wanted to join in the outing. And she had wanted to, so very much. Still sore from the biopsy, she'd forced herself here. Determined to embrace the world.

A loose but elegant navy dress clung to her body, positioned just right to hide the scars.

Adelaide tossed her head, easing herself onto the first step of the pool. A wicked grin warmed her eyes. "We should go lingerie shopping."

"What?" The suggestion snapped Fiona back into the moment. Lingerie shopping would be pretty damn difficult in her state.

Swirling her foot in the water, Adelaide continued, "The new bride will need new lacies. We can call it an impromptu lingerie shower." She whipped out a gold credit card. "Lunch is on me."

Erika's rich peal of laughter resonated on the patio. "I am getting very big very fast. I will not be able to wear the underthings long."

Adelaide winked, emerging from the pool to sit next to Erika. "If you're doing it right, he'll tear them off your body and you'll only be able to wear them once."

A faint blush colored Erika's snow-pale skin.

One of the linebackers' wives spoke in a low rasp. Macie's gray-streaked auburn hair framed her angular face, her crow's-feet crinkling as she sipped on a bottle of water. "I wore bikini panties under my belly for the whole pregnancy."

"I wore thigh-high stockings and a cute little thong. Drove my man wild."

Adelaide nudged Erika with her shoulder. "I've got one! This isn't pregnancy related, but Dempsey goes nuts when I wear these black strappy heels. Does it every time. I'm half inclined to think they are magic."

Erika's moonlight-blond hair rippled as she laughed, and then put her hand to her stomach. "Fiona? So spill. What does that sexy man of yours like you to wear?"

Adelaide turned to face Fiona, brows raised in anticipation.

How to answer that? Sitting up, she choked on the words. Nothing came to her lips.

The stress of the past few months had taken an additional toll on Fiona. She'd unintentionally lost weight. What she hadn't realized was how much weight.

As she shrugged, attempting to brush the question off, the shoulder of her dress slipped down her arm.

Revealing the bandage from the biopsy. And the very edge of the scar just under her breast line from the mastectomy and reconstruction.

The laughter from the other wives stopped. All attention and eyes rested on her.

There was no use in pretending anymore. The charade had finally bested her. In vague horror, she watched their gazes trail from her torso to her face. Watched the transformation of pity in their eyes.

"When? How did no one know?" Erika breathed, rising to her feet. With slow, waddling movements, she made her way to Fiona's side. Sitting down with royal poise, Erika searched Fiona's face while the other team wives stayed diplomatically silent.

"We didn't want anyone to know. We just...took one of our trips and had the surgery done."

Adelaide plopped on her other side, putting a hand on Fiona's back. She ran her hand in small circles up and down her back. "But you have this whole big family here that would have wanted to be there for you. I know they would. The team family, too."

Flashes of her childhood drama and trauma scrolled through her mind. Somehow containing the pain and emotion had seemed easier this time. Had she been wrong? She didn't know. She only knew she and Henri had made the best decision they could at the time. "I'm not certain how to explain it other than to say so much of our lives was in the spotlight, we just wanted to crawl off and be alone."

"Did that help?" Leave it to Erika to be direct. But Fiona preferred that to being treated like a glass mannequin. Looking back and forth from Adelaide to Erika, Fiona noticed that they didn't seem to feel pity. Just concern.

"I thought so at the time. But now I think it could have helped Henri to talk to his brothers. Even if their advice stunk, just to lean on them. Maybe I was being selfish."

Adelaide's voice came out like a wind-tossed whisper. "How so?"

"Wanting him all to myself. I had no one else." She rubbed her temple. "I never really thought of it that way until now." Her eyes stung with tears and regret.

Giving her hands a quick squeeze and a gentle smile, Erika asked, "So you made the decision all on your own to keep it quiet?"

A dark laugh escaped Fiona's lips. "Sounds like you already know the answer to that one. Henri was emphatic about not wanting the press involved. He wanted things quietly handled."

"Even kept from family?" Adelaide asked in a quiet voice. "That was your decision to make. I'm just sorry we didn't provide the support we all would have wanted to give you both."

Fiona had been so concerned with handling this discreetly, she had never stopped to consider what Henri might have needed. So focused on her own needs, on her own wounds, she had been blinded.

In this small moment, as the afternoon sun streamed onto the pool patio, she began to understand that she had deeply hurt Henri. Which was the one thing she had been desperately trying to avoid doing.

The world started spinning. She felt distant from her surroundings. Had she really made the wrong choices?

Ten

"I owe you an apology," Fiona said softly as she stepped into Henri's room in his childhood home at the Reynaud family compound. Not the home they shared on the lake. For whatever reason, Henri had chosen to stay at Gervais's house. It had been tough to find him, but she'd tracked him down.

Now she wondered if that was wise, but there was no leaving.

She felt as if he'd put as much distance between them as he could by coming here, staying under his brother's roof instead of at their second home just up the lane. Could it have something to do with the fact they'd once lived there together? Or maybe it was the nursery they'd decorated for the child they'd lost—a room they'd never changed back. Her throat grew tight, so she blocked that thought. Maybe here was best after all.

Heart pounding, she stepped across the threshold, eyes still adjusting from the bright sun of the fall day.

Blinking slowly, she scanned the room.

The small suite, filled with trophies and photographs of her husband's high school and college careers, felt like a shrine to Henri's past. She hadn't set foot in here for a long time, but she'd always been fond of the large, gold-framed photograph of the Reynaud brothers and Grandpa Leon. The brothers had all still been in high school at the time of the photograph, and Grandpa Leon had had plenty of energy then.

The photograph pulled at her already raw heart. Refusing to become sidetracked by Grandpa Leon's state, she pressed on into the room, leaning on one of the oak poles of the four-poster bed. Henri's eyes stayed fixed on the bed where his suitcase lay open. With a sigh, he yanked another shirt from the suitcase and slung it into an open dresser drawer. Without looking at her, he asked, "How are you feeling?"

Apparently he wasn't in the mood for an apology. Sitting on the edge of the bed, she felt awkward, as if she was forcing her way into this space.

But she had to try. "A little sore but otherwise okay. I didn't even have to take a pain pill today."

"Glad to hear that. I hope you're resting enough," he said in a quiet voice, almost a monotone. Noncommittal.

"It was a biopsy. I'll be fine."

"Just be careful." For the first time since she'd walked into the room, he looked at her. His dark eyes were full of concern.

"In case I need to be prepared for something worse?"

He shrugged, leaning against the dresser. The subtle pressure caused one of his childhood baseball trophies to shift. "You're the one who said that. Not me."

He picked up an old football off the dresser. It was signed by all of his college teammates. Tossing it lightly from one hand to another, he grimaced.

Putting her fingertips to her lips, she took a moment to compose her thoughts, noting the hurt in Henri's expression.

"And that's why I'm here to say I'm sorry for not telling you about the lump and the procedure. Even though we're separated, we're still married. We share an intense history."

"Thank you for acknowledging that." As he folded his arms across his chest with the football still clutched in one hand, she noted the tension in his clenched jaw.

"You've been kind. You've been understanding. You deserve better than the way I treated you."

"You've been through a lot. I understand that." He set the ball down carefully on the dresser again.

"Please take this in the spirit intended, but it's damn hard to be married to the perfect man."

Henri let out a choked laugh, dark hair catching the glow of the lights. "I'm not sure what spirit to take that in at all—and I'm far from perfect. Just ask my brothers."

Her head to the side, she linked her hand with his. "So you'll accept my apology for not telling you about the biopsy?"

"I'm still upset, but yes, I can see that you're sorry..." His voice trailed off and he looked down.

"But?"

"But I'm certain you wouldn't do things differently. Even though you're sorry, you would still shut me out."

He held up a hand. "Don't say anything either way to agree or deny."

He hauled the suitcase off the bed, headed to the ornate closet door. Etched molding that resembled Grecian columns framed the door. Whenever she came here, the details always caught her off guard. Every visit yielded a new dimension of awareness. She'd lived in their Italianate monstrosity across the road. She should have been able to call all this home, but when had she ever taken the time to settle in?

That lack of awareness, it seemed, extended to her understanding of Henri. Now, as he put the empty suitcase in the closet, she began to understand his point of view a bit more clearly.

"We have problems. Big problems. Obviously. I just want us to find peace."

"I agree." He turned to take her by the shoulders, his whole hulking body radiating pain. "You'll be sure to tell me the second you know the results of the biopsy?"

"Of course. Right away." And she could feel how much he cared, really cared. That tore at her, left her feeling conflicted all over again. Just when she was sure she could walk away, doubts plagued her as she felt how much he cared for her. How deeply she was affected by him.

She stroked her hand over his hair, sketching her fingers along the thick, coarse strands. "I truly am sorry I hurt you. I wish our lives could have been easier. That we didn't have to face biopsies and infertility."

"Life isn't guaranteed to be easy." He leaned into her touch.

"I don't know if things would have been smoother if we were chasing a cute little toddler around now."

The tears of loss and regret stung. "A little girl with your brown eyes and feet that never stop because she loves carrying around your football."

"Fiona, you're killing me here." He put his arms around her, careful to avoid her left side.

She let herself enjoy the warmth of his embrace. She couldn't bring herself to step away. Keeping distance between them the past months had been torture and right now she couldn't recall why she had to.

Pressing her ear against his chest over the steady beat of his heart, she slid her arms around his waist. She took in the musky smell of his soap and a scent that was 100 percent Henri. Her husband. Her man.

She heard the shift in his breathing at the same time her own body kindled to life. She shouldn't be feeling this way right now. Turned on. Aching to make sweet tender love to him.

Henri nuzzled her hair. "You should rest."

Angling back, she met his gaze dead-on. "I don't want to sleep. I want you to make love to me. Here. Now. No thinking about tomorrow or what we'll say after. Let's be together—"

He kissed her silent, once, twice, holding the kiss for an instant before speaking against her mouth. "You won't hear an argument from me. I want you. Always. Anywhere, anytime."

He walked her back toward the bed, sealing his lips to hers every step of the way until her legs bumped the footboard. He angled her back onto the mattress, cradling her body with arms so strong, so gentle. She sank into the puffy comforter, reaching for Henri only to have him drop to his knees at the foot of the bed. He bunched her skirt up an inch at a time, nibbling

along the inside of her left leg, stroking her other leg
with his hand.

He made his way higher. Higher still. Until…

Her head pushed back into the bed as she sighed in
anticipation. His breath puffed against the lacy silk of
her panties, warming her.

"Lovely," he murmured.

"I went shopping."

"I was talking about you." He skimmed the panties off and his mouth found her, pressing an intimate
kiss to the core of her.

She felt his hum of appreciation against her skin.
She grabbed fistfuls of the blanket and twisted, pleasure sparking through her. His tongue stroked, cir-
cled, teased at the tight bundle of nerves until her head
thrashed restlessly against the bed. Her heels dug into
his back, anchoring him, but also anchoring herself in
this oh-so-personal moment. She ached for completion. And one flick at a time he drove her to the edge
of release, backed off, then brought her even closer,
again and again until she demanded he finish, now,
yes, now… And he listened with delicious attention
to her need.

Gasps of bliss and, ah, release filled the air as ripple after ripple of pleasure shuddered through her. Her
back bowed upward and her fingers slid down to comb
through his hair as he eased her through the last ves-
tiges of her orgasm.

Gently, he slid her legs from his shoulders and
smoothed her dress back into place. He stretched out
beside her, carrying them both up to recline against
the pillows.

She traced her fingers along his T-shirt. "That was

amazing. Thank you. This may sound obvious, but it feels so good to feel good right now."

"That was my intent."

She pressed her mouth to his. "I want us both to feel good again. Make love to me."

"But you're recovering…"

"There's no reason we can't have sex as long as you're gentle." A smile tugged at her lips. "Ironic and a little funny, but I'm actually asking you to treat me like spun glass."

"I'll take you any way I can have you, lady. You're perfect, you know that, right?" He pressed kisses against the curve of her neck.

"Far from it, but thank you." She angled her head to give him easier access.

"I mean it. You're beautiful and giving and smart." His hands moved reverently over her long dark hair, skimming low, lower still and then back up again to rest on her shoulders.

"What brought this on?" She touched his face, reveling in his stubble, in his dark eyes.

"I just wanted to make sure you know. I think I get so caught up in gestures, I forget to give you the words." Gentle fingers traveled from her lips to her neck, causing shivers to run wildly down her spine. Sparks lit her nerves, the tingling then gathering at her core.

"Well, thank you for those lovely words. I appreciate it. I do understand that I am not defined by my breasts," she said.

Kissing her collarbone, he pulled her flush against him. "I'm glad you realize that."

Her heart filled again with something that felt like hope.

* * *

With Fiona asleep in his bed, he felt better than he had in weeks. Hell, better than he had in months. The scent of her on his linens was something he didn't take for granted. He'd missed this. Missed her. And looked forward to devoting even more attention to persuading her to stay right here.

But still…he felt compelled to move. To walk about the house to process the 180-degree change he saw in Fiona.

He slid out of the silk bedsheets, his feet landing on cool marble tile. On tiptoes, he made his way out of the room.

When was the last time he'd spent any time out at the lake, trying to ferret out an answer to a complex problem? He couldn't remember. He and Fiona had spent so much time trying to give themselves privacy, he'd forgotten what it was like to share space with his brothers. To ask for help.

Now, staying in this wing of his childhood home, he could see his older brother's stamp on the place. He'd made changes to personalize the home, yet he'd kept so many things from their past, too. Leaving Henri's old bedroom untouched had been a welcome surprise.

For the most part, he barely registered the mammoth house anymore. Greek Revival wasn't his style—it felt too rigid and restrictive. As he walked through the house, he found himself appreciating the quirky charm of his home in the Garden District. The eclectic Victorian space he and Fiona had reconstructed.

Needing to talk, he searched for his brother. After all, Gervais had pushed him down this path by sending his fiancée, Erika, to deliver flowers to Fiona.

Catching sight of his brother's silhouette by the pool, Henri opened the sliding glass door. Gervais stood, back to the house, on the path that led from the pool to the dock.

Gervais's shoulders were slumped. Heavy as the boughs of the live oak trees. Fragrant ginger and bushes lined the paths around the pool, next to a round fire pit surrounded by a low wall of flat rocks. A glider swing with a seat as big as a full-size bed anchored the space, which was draped in breezy white gauze threaded with a few tiny twinkly lights overhead.

His brother's hands were linked behind his back. As Henri drew closer, he could see that Gervais was squeezing his hands so tight they were turning white.

Surveying the landscape in front of them, Henri watched the dying light bathe the wooden dock in rich oranges. At the end of the dock, the pontoon boat was hoisted out of the water. They'd spent many nights out on that pontoon boat—and the yacht off to the left— when they were younger. As he looked at the pontoon boat, he felt a wave of nostalgia wash over him. Things felt simpler then. But he knew that wasn't actually true. Nothing about his family had ever been simple.

These past few months had been a strain on Henri's relationship with his family. Everything between his brothers and him had been placed on autopilot. Nods and lies became the default modes of communication.

Had those months of evading serious conversation come at the high cost of neglecting to see that his brother had been struggling? Impending marriage and managing the team were enough to test anyone, even his collected and cool older brother.

Henri tried to imagine what was on Gervais's mind:

owning the New Orleans Hurricanes, having a winning season, even what was going on with their baby brother Jean-Pierre's career as a New York quarterback.

And smack-dab in the middle of all that, Gervais was trying to plan a wedding to a princess and keep it out of the public eye, all while facing fatherhood. And Dempsey was engaged. Life was moving forward at full force.

"What are you doing down here?" Henri asked.

"Reliving the old days." Gervais's chest expanded as he breathed deeply. A football lay at his feet. He gave it a shove with his shoe.

"Do you miss it?" Henri gestured to the pigskin.

"Sure I miss playing sometimes. But I'm not you, living and breathing for the game. Honestly. I like being the brains behind the larger operation."

"Impending marriage and fatherhood has made you philosophical."

Gervais shook his head. "Practical. Focused."

"I'm so damn tired of people questioning my focus."

"People?" Cocking his head to the side, Gervais stared at his brother. It was a knowing kind of glance, one that chided him to be more specific.

"My family." He practically spat the words from his mouth.

"You *are* staring at a possible divorce." Such a blunt statement. As if Henri wasn't aware of the state of his marriage.

"So are half the guys out there playing."

"But you love your wife."

Henri stared hard at the lake, his voice growing quiet, the words feeling like ash as he spoke them. "I thought I did."

"You do, you big idiot."

Henri shoved Gervais's shoulder. "I hate it when you pull the wise big brother act."

"Then do something about it—you're the Bayou Bomber, for God's sake. You run the Hurricanes' offense from the quarterback position, slinging record-setting pass yardage with an arm destined for the Hall of Fame. You can't do better than this in your personal life?"

Henri let out a bitter laugh. "Brother, no offense. But this marriage thing is a helluva lot harder than it looks."

Gervais scooped up the football and tossed it to him. "Our family is too quick to anger and rifts."

"What are you talking about? We're tight." He stepped back, putting some distance between them before flinging the football back at his brother.

"Seriously? Are you delusional?" Gervais caught the pigskin, surprise coloring his face.

"Look at us now." Henri gestured between them and to the sprawling buildings of the family property.

"Look at our history," Gervais retorted. "Our dad didn't speak to the mother of his son for over a decade. We find out we have a brother we never knew about and Mom leaves, never to be heard from again. We have a brother in New York who barely graces our doorstep unless we're in crisis. We have one uncle who doesn't speak to us at all. And another in Texas who only shows up to support his son who plays on the team. This family doesn't have a problem cutting and running."

"I guess when you put it that way, it doesn't sound like a close-knit clan." Henri mused over his brother's words, balancing them against the security their lake-side spread had always given him. The mere presence of the Reynaud family homestead had anchored him, made him believe they were close and as stable as the Greek Revival construction. Gervais's words shook his foundation.

"Families have their problems, sure, but ours has more than a few. And I just don't want to see you fall victim to the pattern of cutting someone off rather than working through the tough stuff."

"You're referring to Fiona and me." Nodding in understanding, he tossed the football again.

"Yes, I am. You two are good together. Quite frankly, this break scares the hell out of me as I look at tying the knot myself. You two were the perfect couple."

"There's no such thing as perfect."

"Truth. So why are you expecting perfection?" Gervais lobbed more than just the football at Henri that time.

"Who says I'm the one who wants the divorce?" Gervais was out of line. Henri didn't want a divorce, didn't want things between Fiona and him to be over. His passion burned for her and her alone. Life without her... It was an impossible thought for him to even finish.

"If she's the one who wants to walk, then why aren't you fighting for her?"

"I'm giving her space." Space had been what she wanted.

"Space... Like I said, our family gives space all too easily." Gervais slammed the football to the ground, turning away from Henri to look at the compound.

His philosophical brother struck a chord in Henri. His words reverberated in his chest, stirring a renewed commitment to winning Fiona's mind, body and soul. Passion had never been a problem for him and Fiona. That burned bright and true. But this was more than getting her back into his bed. He wanted her back in his life. Full time.

He refused to be another Reynaud who cut and run.

She'd been dreaming about Henri.

In Fiona's imagination, they'd been together in Seattle, exploring the city's art district during one of the Hurricanes' trips to the West Coast. It had been the early days of their marriage, and they'd run through the rain to dart from one private studio to the next, trying to meet some of the city's up-and-coming artists just for the fun of it.

In the car on the way back to the hotel, they'd been sopping wet and laughing. Kissing. Touching with a feverish urgency. Almost as if they'd known their time together was limited and they needed to live on fast-forward.

Why hadn't she tried to slow things down? To build the bond that they'd need to get them through a lifetime instead of floating on that high of incredible physical intimacy?

Even as she thought it in her hazy dreams, she became aware of a strong hand on her hip. Stroking. Rubbing.

Alertness came to her slowly. Or maybe she just didn't mind lingering in that dreamy world between wakefulness and sleep. The real world had disappointed her enough times in the past year and a half.

She would gladly take her touches with her eyes closed for just a little while longer.

Her body hummed to life at Henri's urging, skin shivering with awareness at his caress.

"Fiona." Her husband breathed her name in a sigh that tickled along her bare neck right before he kissed her there.

Slowly. Thoroughly.

What was it about a kiss on the neck that could drive a woman wild? she wondered. Or was it only Henri's kisses that could turn her inside out like this?

Still lying on her side, she reached for him, knowing where he'd be. She palmed his rock-hard chest. He was so warm. So strong.

"Open your eyes." His soft command made her smile.

"Since when do you give orders in bed?" she teased, keeping her eyes closed.

"Since I need you to see me." His words, spoken with a starkness she hadn't expected, forced her eyes open.

"Is everything all right?" She moved her hand from his chest to his face, her eyes adjusting to the last rays of daylight filtering in through the blinds.

She'd napped for longer than she realized.

"Yes. I just needed to see you." He skimmed his hand up her side, following the curve of her waist to bring her closer to him in the bed.

"You're sure?" She crept closer still, remembering how good she'd felt in her dream. No, how good he'd made her feel just a few hours ago before she'd fallen asleep.

"Positive. I just want you to know I'm here." He dipped a kiss into the hollow behind her ear.

She sensed more at work, but she was content to lose herself in the moment. In the touches she'd denied herself for too long. No matter what the future held for her and Henri, she wanted to savor these moments in a way she hadn't known to do in the past. For too long, she'd been focused on their problems. For now, she wanted to remember the things they'd done well.

The things that made them both happy.

Threading her fingers through his hair, she sifted through to his scalp, down to his neck and over his powerful shoulders. He halted her touch midway down his arm. He gripped her hand to kiss her wrist and then continue down the inside of her forearm, surprising her with how ticklish she was there.

Their shared laughter felt like a rare gift, the moment so oddly poignant she wasn't sure if she should cry or jump him. Their eyes met. Held.

And she had her answer.

She needed this. Him. Melting into his arms, she kissed him, nipping his lower lip and stroking his tongue with growing urgency. He stripped her naked, removing every barrier between them while she poured all the longing of the last months into that kiss. His hands molded her gently, cruising over her curves and paying homage to every inch of her that wasn't in pain.

"I've missed you." He said it so softly she thought it was her own thought for a moment. "I know I've said it before, but I mean it."

"I know. Me, too," she admitted, glancing up to meet his eyes. Needing to say the words, too. "I've missed you, just being together, so much."

That's why she needed him so much right now.

He must have understood—of course he understood, since he knew her so damn well—because he shifted her thighs with his knee. He made a place for himself, gripping her hips and steering her where he wanted her. Close to him. So close.

She was ready for him, but he took his time brushing featherlight caresses up the hot, needy center of her until she had to threaten him with dire sexual payback if he didn't come inside her.

She could feel his smile against her mouth when he kissed her and the heat of him nudged inside her. His smile faded when she thrust her hips hard into his, taking all of him and holding him tight. She could feel his heart pound hard and fast against her chest on the right side where he allowed himself to make contact with her.

Arms looped around his neck, she trusted him with her body. Knew he'd be careful with her and make her feel amazing at the same time.

And oh, did he deliver.

With his powerful thrust, he could have delivered heart-stopping pleasure to her all night long. He was tireless in pursuit of her pleasure. And while normally she liked to ensure he was every bit as swept away as her, tonight she simply let the desire build. Allowed the sensations to build however he wanted. Gave herself over to him completely.

"Henri." She whispered his name more than once as he took her to one dizzying high after another.

She clung to him, raining kisses down his impossibly strong torso, savoring the shift of muscle beneath her hands with his every movement.

When he finally reached that point of no return, she met his gaze again, remembering that he wanted her to see him.

What she saw sent her crashing into blissful completion as much as any skillful touch. Wave after wave of pleasure shuddered through her, undulating over her body. She felt his release, too, not just inside her, but under her hands as his back bowed and his muscles tensed.

She held him for a long time afterward, stroking his hair and remembering every moment they'd spent together. But most of all, she thought about what she'd seen in his eyes in that shattering moment before she'd hit her peak.

Her husband still loved her. Deeply.

And she was terrified of what that meant for both of them.

Eleven

Between her jumbled feelings for Henri and waiting for her biopsy results, the past days getting ready for the fund-raiser had zipped by in a blur of emotion. She'd spent every spare moment attending to different details. Making sure the event would go off without a hitch.

Making sure she didn't have time to think about the confusing mess she'd made of her life.

The lingering aftereffects of her biopsy still caused a dull ache in her chest and throughout her shoulder. The pain didn't slow her down, though. Her recent diagnosis of the cancer gene filled Fiona with a renewed sense of commitment to the cause. This event wasn't just in memory of her mother, aunt and grandmother. No, Fiona needed this event to work—to outperform any event she'd ever done—because she needed, down to her bones, to be a part of eradicating this disease that took too much from people and their families.

So she'd spent hours on the phone, personally reaching out to all her contacts to woo them into sponsoring the event. She found creative ways to pay for a memorable gala without taking an extra penny from the client's budget. No detail was too small for her to tackle full force.

She couldn't deny that another factor contributed to her increased productivity. Henri. Her failing marriage. The reality of life without him.

The thoughts were too real, too hard for her to deal with. Fiona threw herself into the fund-raiser because it filled her with purpose and direction. Things she desperately needed in her life right now.

After another day of dogged dedication, Fiona felt suffocated by the walls of her lonely home. It was time to get some fresh air and, she did need to get some paperwork she'd left at the Reynaud compound.

Not that she was looking for an excuse to run into Henri.

A quick drive later, she arrived at the sprawling cluster of buildings…the Greek Revival main house, the Italianate home, the carriage house, the boathouse…the dock.

Her gaze snagged on a figure at the end of the dock. Gramps sat on the bench overlooking the water, and while she knew he was likely fine, she also worried about him wandering off in a fog.

She set out toward the dock and the water, each step closer filling her lungs with the familiar scents of this place that had once been her home. The lake air had a way of breathing life into her.

The Friday event would irrevocably change the course of her life. And Henri's. As much as it pained her, she knew it was time to cut the ties between them. She could not—no, she would not—be the source of pain for him anymore. He deserved more. He deserved children and a wife who wasn't so sickly. Leaving would shelter his heart from any additional pain if those results—due any time now—turned out for the worst.

Though Henri had wanted her to stay with him through the rest of the season, she couldn't put them both through that. Too much pain. Too much exposure to the electric passion that hummed between them. And after the last few days…well, she couldn't lead either of them on like that.

After the charity event on Friday, Fiona would create her own timetable for leaving Henri. One that minimized damage to both of them.

A season of difficult choices was upon her. Henri planned on attending the event on Friday before leaving Saturday for Indianapolis, where he'd play his Sunday game. The running assumption was that she'd join him, take her place in the wives' section of the stands.

But maybe…maybe the better call came in the form of a clean break after the event. Leaving him to travel alone.

Alone?

Revulsion settled in the pit of her stomach. Alone. Could she really let him be unsupported during a season that could finally be the one he deserved? A season that might allow him to achieve all his professional dreams? As he'd pointed out, it wasn't just his dreams that were on the line this year, either. So many of the Reynauds were bound up in the Hurricanes' future. Could she live with herself if she was the cause of their championship run falling apart?

Before she could explore the ramifications of her idea, she got to Grandpa Leon. He clutched a glass of juice and balanced on his lap a dinner plate that contained specks of spiced sausage and rice.

His state continued to shock Fiona. Every time she saw him, he looked less and less like himself. The disease seemed to steal more than just his mind. The effects were rendered visible on his skin, his face. Even his smile had shifted, changed.

Glancing at her, he motioned for Fiona to sit next to him. "The boys used to like boating. But I don't see them use the yacht that often. Or maybe I am forgetting that, too. It just seems everyone is so busy working."

Sitting down beside him, she laid a hand on his tissue-paper-thin skin. "You would be right about that."

"I used to work, too. A lot." Grandpa Leon's sight turned inward. Fiona wondered what he remembered in this moment. If they were real memories or imagined.

"Yes, sir, you did."

"So I guess I'm to blame." Taking a swig of his juice, he spoke into his crystal glass.

Fiona shook her head, gathering her hair in her fist and pulling it over her shoulder. Grandpa Leon had stepped up for Henri and his brothers. Set a good example about the value of hard work and family. "They're adults. We all are. We make our own choices."

Flashing her a dentureless smile, he tapped her temple. "I've always liked you. When I remember who you are, of course."

"And I adore your sense of humor in the face of what has to be... Well, I enjoy your humor."

"Thank you, dear." His gaze returned out toward the yacht. Toward the past and what had been. Swirling around the last few drops of his juice, he let out a small sigh.

"Could I get you a jacket or a pillow?" she asked just as she saw Henri walking toward them. Her stomach twisted into knots and she wanted to run into his arms, but that would mean giving him answers to questions she wasn't ready to face yet.

Gramps extended his juice glass, staring absently ahead. "Just more juice."

Springing to her feet, she grabbed the glass from him and made fast tracks for the house, racing past Henri.

So much for a conversation with Fiona. She was dodging him like the plague.

Though Henri knew Fiona was busy with her fundraiser, he felt that her disappearing act over these past few days had more to do with what was unresolved between them.

Henri had caught sight of her from the pool patio, sitting with his grandfather, looking out on the lake. She'd always been so good with Grandpa Leon. Nurturing. Kind. And as the disease claimed more and more of his memory, Fiona never lost her temper, but took it in stride, displaying patience even saints would envy.

Making his way out to her, Henri felt anticipation quicken his steps. She'd practically run into him, glass in hand. Her face was solemn, and she was quiet as she made her way back to the house.

Grandpa Leon turned his head, looking over his shoulder at Henri. Recognition washed over his expression.

Good. These days, Grandpa Leon's ability to process who was in front of him had waned. To be recognized was a rare blessing.

Gramps clapped Henri on the back as he sat down. "Nice figure on your girlfriend there, Christophe."

Henri's stomach fell. Watching his grandfather grasp at memories would never become easy. Grandpa Leon thought he was Christophe, his father's brother.

The Texas branch of the family was deeply involved in the Reynaud shipping empire and the cruise ship business. They owned an island off Galveston that was a self-sustaining working ranch and an optional stop on many of their cruise itineraries. Guests could ride horseback on the gulf beaches or take part in one of the farm-to-table feasts that made use of the organically grown vegetables. They hadn't visited their Texas cousins in years due to a family rift. Leon had publicly cut his oldest son, Christophe, out of his will long ago, but Uncle Christophe still retained his title as a vice president of global operations and, along with his oldest son, was very much a part of the family business.

Grandpa Leon's greeting was a small slipup. It didn't mean anything. Henri coughed, stepping closer to his grandfather. He scratched the back of his neck, hoping his grandfather would recognize him now. "Um, thank you."

Leon tapped Henri's ring finger. "You're married?

Married men shouldn't have a piece on the side. It's not right."

Offering a small smile, he sat down next to his grandfather. "Grandpa, I'm Henri, and Fiona's my wife."

Fog settled on his grandfather. He pursed his lips, weighing the information. Looking down at his feet, he shook his head. "Oh, right. Of course you are, and she is. I just never expected you to go for the kind who've, um, had surgical embellishments."

"I'm not sure what you're talking about."

Grandpa Leon's eyebrows shot up. Cocking his head to the right, he gestured to his chest and lifted upward a hint.

Just in time for Fiona to come back with his re-filled juice.

Henri's voice fell low. "How do you know that?"

"I have a keen eye for the finer things in life. I just am not so sure why such an already perfect woman would alter anything about herself."

Handing the glass to Henri, Fiona leaned in to kiss Grandpa Leon's cheek. "Grandpa, you're amazing. Love you."

The older man reached up to touch the side of her face. Henri saw how the simplest movements tired his grandfather.

Dropping his hand away from Fiona, Grandpa Leon peered back and forth between Fiona and Henri. He pursed his dry lips.

Handing his grandfather the glass of juice, Henri looked at his wife, trying to ferret out what she was thinking.

Grandpa Leon took a big swig of his juice and

popped his lips. Shakily, he rose to his feet, stretching his arms out above him.

"You two kids have fun. *Jeopardy* will be on soon and I can't miss that." He winked at Henri, shuffling toward the house.

"Do you need help, Grandpa?" Henri asked earnestly.

Waving Henri off, Grandpa Leon shook his head. "No. No. You two stay here. Enjoy the sunset."

As Leon walked to the house, Fiona made her way to the dock. Sitting on the edge, she let her bare feet dangle over the water, swinging them to unheard music.

Henri strode over to join her. He was itching to speak to her. To win her back still, even though she'd been avoiding him over the last few days.

Taking a seat next to her, he remembered all the times they'd sat here when they were first married. They'd talk here for hours. About literature and art and football. Everything.

Fiona twisted her rope of long dark hair draped over her shoulder. "How strange that your grandfather knew I'd had surgery all this time and never said a word. I might have expected a man to notice if I'd opted for larger, but since I went down a cup size... I'm just surprised."

"You and I instituted the code of silence on this. Maybe he sensed that, too." His grandfather had always been intuitive, if a bit eccentric.

Leon hadn't given Henri and his brothers the most traditional upbringing once he'd stepped in to take charge of his four rowdy grandsons, but he understood boys. He'd brought a fifties-era Harley-Davidson to the Texas ranch to give them a lesson in engine rebuilding. The motorcycle had been in crates when he bought the beat-up old thing. By the end of the summer they'd reveled in seeing how fast it would race on the private ranch roads. They'd even collected a lot of bruises along the way.

Memories of his youth and his grandfather flooded him. Watching as Alzheimer's consumed Grandpa Leon's mind tore at Henri. It was as if the lines connecting the flowchart of Grandpa Leon's memories had been erased.

"All this time I thought I was the one holding back. But it's you, too. You're scared," Henri said to Fiona.

"I meet with the doctor tomorrow. I'll know one way or another. Odds really are that it's nothing."

"I want to be there…" He paused. "But I can see in your eyes I'm not welcome."

"It's not that. I'm just not sure I can…" She shook her head. "Hell, I don't know. I just need to do this on my own."

Silence pooled around them, filling the spaces between them. It cut deeper than any fight or argument they'd had.

At least when they were fighting, he felt a connection. That their relationship had a chance because there was an active struggle. This silence felt like a killing blow.

As the sun sank farther into the lake horizon, he felt the weight of their situation sink onto his shoulders. He was losing her.

Pink balloons covered the entire ceiling of the new wing of the hospital soon to open as an updated children's oncology floor. Fiona clutched a glass of champagne, taking in the mass of people that flooded the ward.

Success. Her biggest one yet. Despite the tiny budget and last-minute assignment, the event was packed. In one corner, people bid on silent auction items, which were always a strong source of donations at charity events. A few casino games provided more entertainment and allowed attendees to contribute while having fun.

But the event was mostly family oriented. Nearby, a troupe of storytellers in elaborate costumes held the attention of a glitzed-out crowd. She watched the emotions play out on the faces of the audience.

Across the room from her, Henri handed out footballs signed by the entire Hurricanes team. She watched the way the women in the crowd ogled him. A surge of jealousy sank into her veins.

The event should make her feel fulfilled. At the very least, accomplished. But as she surveyed the pianist and TV star-turned-pop singer Daisy Dani, she felt hollow. She smoothed her crepe skirt, fingers catching on the sequins that outlined a paisley pattern that managed to be elegant and bohemian at the same time. While the deep purple skirt shone with metallic highlights, the dark silk blouse on top was simple and secure. No more shoulder-baring costume mishaps for her.

Hearing Henri's laugh from across the room ignited her feet to move. Things had been strange between them over the past few days. A new sort of strain had settled between them. She'd tried texting him earlier, but phones were forbidden during practice.

The results of her biopsy had come in today. She'd

promised to let him know the results and she had. Right away.

The biopsy had revealed nothing. No cancer. Such news ought to fill her with relief and promise, but the risk of the cancer gene would always be part of her existence. Just like her scars. Permanent marks on her mind and body.

Fiona had told Henri via text that she was in the clear. Everything from the test had come back normal. No reason to worry.

As she made her way to Henri, she bumped into the doctor who had asked her out. Had that really only been a few weeks ago?

So much had changed since her last fund-raiser. Her relationship with Henri had cooled and heated…and now? Well, now it was an utter mess.

Things with the doctor were cordial, platonic. At least on her end. Avoiding a drawn-out conversation, she almost couldn't believe her eyes.

She blinked, stunned. Jean-Pierre had arrived at the party. He and Henri hadn't exchanged more than a few words in months. Things in the family had been strained since Jean-Pierre had left New Orleans. But having him show up added to the pro ball appeal of the event, and would give the fund-raising a generous boost.

As the youngest Reynaud, Jean-Pierre had inherited his love of the game from his father and his grandfather, the same as his brothers. But Jean-Pierre had gone to college playing the quarterback position, the same as Henri. And since Jean-Pierre wasn't the kind of man to play in a brother's shadow, he hadn't wanted a spot on the Hurricanes. He was a starter and an elite player. When the New York Gladiators had made him an offer, he'd taken it.

Fiona shouldered through the masses of people to her brother-in-law.

"Jean-Pierre, how did you know we could use the extra help for this? It's wonderful to see you, but why are you here?"

"Henri told me you had to salvage this event so he called me." He grinned, leaning in to give her a hug and a kiss on her cheek. "Access to the family's private plane has its perks. I had some time, so I was able to swing it."

"Thank you." She was touched. Not just by Jean-Pierre's quick flight and visit, but that Henri had thought to ask him.

Jean-Pierre acknowledged greetings from a few friends, and now the whole room was buzzing with all the star power. When his fans had shuffled past, his eyes returned to Fiona's. "Not a problem. The Gladiators' PR guy thought it was a good idea. I'm off to sign a few more autographs. Nice party. You did a great job."

She thanked him again before he melted into the crowd, moving slowly since he was signing autographs as he made his way, shaking hands and making time for everyone who wanted to see him.

With no one else vying for her attention, Fiona edged her way to Henri. He looked so handsome in his tuxedo, as he always did. But she could see the way he stiffened as she approached, as if bracing for the next hit. The tension in his jaw pulsated as she drew near. Hurt still colored his face.

Tugging at his blue shirtsleeve, she leaned into him,

her heavy sterling silver bracelet sliding down her arm. Placing her hand on his chest, she tried to memorize his scent and the way he stood. Pain ached in her joints. Everything would change after this conversation.

She just hoped she'd make it through the hardest conversation she'd ever have.

"Let's step outside. Just us." The words formed on her tongue like a prayer or a plea.

Rather than answering her, he placed his hand on the small of her back. Shivers rolled up her spine as he led them outside. Laughter and music filtered through the doors as they sat on the bench in the garden patio.

In the distance, the night hummed with the sound of expensive cars being parked by the valets. A few feet away, a water feature gurgled and multicolored lights glinted. A few patients who'd been medically cleared to attend were brought out in wheelchairs and chatted with guests. One teen in particular caught her eye, a thin girl with a party hat—a cloth jester cap—on her bald head. Streamers glittered from her chair and her mother leaned down to whisper something while her father set plates of food down on a nearby bench.

Fiona tore her gaze away before the image dragged her under, and focused her attention back on Henri. There was a buzz of activity here, but not the press of a crowd like inside. Here, they could speak privately, seated on another bench, one of the three she'd donated in memory of her mother, her grandmother and her aunt.

Henri's mouth thinned for a moment. She could see the ragged edges of his nerves, the stress she'd caused. The hurt. Her fingers clutched the edges of the stately concrete bench, sturdy, made to survive far longer than her mother had. Her breath hitched as she fought harder to tamp down the tears, the emotion.

Henri gently pried her hand free from the bench—her mother's bench—and linked fingers with her. She tried to hold onto the feel of his rough calluses from years and years of training and practice.

His wedding band glinted in the halo of patio lights. "Thank you for letting me know about the doctor visit. I'm glad the scare's over. And that you're okay."

Chewing her lip, she could only think of this party, everything surrounding her reminding her of what she needed to do no matter how much pain it caused her.

"Except the scare will never be over, Henri. There will always be a next time. You'll worry every time I go for a checkup." Words exploded from her mouth like gunshots. He needed to hear this. Needed to understand everything. "Look at you. Even when I say that now, you look like you're going to throw up."

"Because I care about you, dammit."

"I care about you, too." She couldn't deny the truth any longer. "In fact, I'm still in love with you."

"You love me? Then why the hell are you divorcing me?" he barked, confusion swimming in his dark eyes.

"Because I can see how this is tearing you apart. Even your grandfather sees me as I am. A woman with a high risk of contracting cancer one day. I pray if I do that it will be curable. But I don't know. I do know *I* can live with that possibility." She looked around her, at the patients in the wheelchairs. And she looked at their families with their haunted, exhausted and scared eyes. "But I can't live with watching how afraid it makes you."

"You were fine with us having sex and being together these past few days when you thought it was day by day." He leveled the accusation at her. His gruff voice seemed to shake the night air. "Then, once you had to think about forever, you shut me out."

"That's not fair. You're not listening."

"I am listening. I've been listening. And you know what I hear?" He turned sideways on the bench, drawing his face close to hers. Tucking a loose hair behind her ear, he breathed. "I keep hearing none of this is fair to either one of us."

Desire. Hurt. Longing. The three warring emotions beat in her chest, threatening to disrupt her course of action. But she had to focus on why she was here. To end things before either of them suffered a loss they'd never recover from. She had to be brave, to face this head-on.

Pulling away from his touch, she lowered his hand to his lap. "We shouldn't be discussing this two days before a game. You need to focus."

"Impossible." Resting his forehead on his hand, rubbing his temples, talking more to the ground than to her, he said, "There's never going to be a good time for this conversation."

"Henri, please, what are you hoping to accomplish?"

"To make you admit what we had was real." He tipped his head to look sideways at her. "But you checked out of our relationship."

Tears clogged her throat, even stinging her nose. But she wouldn't cry in front of him. She'd shed so many tears over the mess she'd made of their marriage. "Fine, you wanted this conversation now, we'll have it. I admit it. I can't deal with being married to you. I'm scared as hell, every single day when I wake up, that

I'm going to get sick, and just the thought of you griev-ing over me dying rips my heart out again and again."

Fiona knew how to pick a moment. Art had taught her as much. She knew what leaving looked like. Her mother, her aunt, her grandmother. Knew what it was like to be left behind, to suffer with a loss that rav-aged the bones.

With tender fingers, she stroked the side of his face, tracing the faintest stubble with her fingertips. His lips parted slightly. Leaning into him, she inhaled his cologne and musk. Her lips found his. Pressed a kiss from her soul to his.

Their last kiss.

Twelve

Henri had thought football was his world. Until he met Fiona.

Love for her had slammed into him hard and fast.

As hard and fast as the Indianapolis linebacker plowing toward him—

Damn.

His body hit the ground in a crunch of shoulder pads, grunts and smack talk. Well deserved. He was losing this game for his team. His mind wasn't in the game. Hell, his heart wasn't in it.

Crisp fall air stung his lungs as he viewed the world from the ground. How damn symbolic. Dazed, he blinked into focus. Eyes scanning the crowd, he saw the disappointment on the faces of his teammates after what should have been a straightforward third-down conversion. He clenched his teeth.

This game should have been a simple win for them. The Hurricanes had a better record against better opponents. Their key players were all healthy. But instead of posting big numbers for their team and calling in some guys off the bench, they were fighting to stay in the game, and that was clearly his fault.

The world spun, but not just from the impact of the 230-pound rookie with the speed of a track star. Henri's eyes trailed to the wives' section, where he half expected to see Fiona, decked out in team colors and a scarf.

But she wasn't there. Hadn't bothered to get on the plane. She'd said she was still in love with him and for that precise reason, she needed to leave him.

Nothing made sense anymore.

He'd spent too much time knocked down lately. Pushing himself off the turf, he launched into the air, landing on his feet.

The Hurricanes fans peppered through the crowd cheered as he rose to his feet. At once believing in him and completely oblivious to the metaphorically shaky ground he stood on. They wouldn't cheer if they understood why his game was off.

Brushing the dirt from his shoulder, he started to walk toward his team. But two of the team trainers were already there, ready to help him off the field.

"I'm fine." He waved them off.

He could hear the offensive coordinator in his ear through the microphone in his helmet. "You're off the field, Henri."

"What the hell?" Henri straightened his helmet that had been knocked askew, talking to the trainers and his offensive coach at the same time. "I'm fine."

He could see his brother Dempsey, the head coach, waving him off the field from the sidelines. His backup had already sprinted to the huddle.

Benched? What in the hell would that accomplish? Henri's pride bristled. It was not as if they were punting it away. The Hurricanes were going for it on fourth down, trying to take that yardage he'd failed to grab in the last play.

"You're going to lose if you take me out." He could still recover the game. The tackle left him with new clarity.

Adjusting his ball cap, Dempsey shook his head, eyes firm and impassive as Henri reached his side. "And you're going to risk breaking your damn neck out there. I'm not ending this day with you in the hospital." He shoved his microphone aside to talk to Henri without an audience on their headsets.

Nearby, the offensive coordinator stepped up to run the show as the clock kept ticking.

"So what, I get tackled once and suddenly I'm a candidate for ICU?" Henri barked back, tugging off his helmet to keep this conversation as private as the fishbowl of a stadium would allow.

Dempsey ripped off his own headset, too, turning a shoulder to the field. Away from the inevitable cameras focused on them.

"We both know that's not what's going on here. Fiona isn't here and your rocky marriage has compromised your focus like we all damn well warned you it would. You are getting your ass handed to you out there," Dempsey said flatly.

"To hell with that. I can handle the field," he shouted back at his brother, rage coursing in his veins.

Henri's teammates nearby exchanged glances. Outbursts of emotion weren't his normal MO and no one talked back to the coach—family or not.

Dempsey leveled a glare at him. "This isn't the backyard. And you might want to think about what you say next." He slammed his headset back into place and turned his attention toward the field where the backup QB had just run for the yards they needed.

A much-needed Hurricanes first down and it hadn't come from Henri. He tried to hide his bitterness, knowing damn well a camera would be closing in on his face right about now.

Henri's cousin and Wild Card approached him, providing a wall of shoulders between him and the cameras.

"Hey, man. Just sit out a few. We'll do you proud, brother." Wild Card clapped him on the shoulder, walking out a stinger in his knee from a previous play.

"Yeah, cuz. We're a family here. Let someone else step up and take care of business. You take care of you," his cousin said with his Texas twang. No judgment, no fuss. They were good men. Good friends.

Deep down, Henri knew that. He seethed anyway.

Sitting on the bench, he watched his second family execute play after play. They moved like an extension of each other. Synced. In tune.

The longer he sat on the bench, the more Dempsey's words rang true. Dempsey had called it. Henri's performance had been poor. He'd been asking for an injury, asking to feel something other than numb.

Pulling him from the game was the right call. But then, Dempsey wasn't calling the plays because he was a novice. His older half brother had as much at stake this season as he did. More, maybe.

Henri had to get his head together for real. Because in marriage, he didn't have any backup. It was just him and he was screwing it up big-time. This was about more than football. It was about his wife. His life.

His love.

Guilt flooded through Fiona.

She should have gone to Henri's game. He'd come to her fund-raiser and, yes, the night had ended with a fight. The worst kind. The forever kind.

The longer she spent alone with her ice cream in her garden, the more she realized she needed to talk to him. She needed to shake him out of his family's habit of cutting people off—his family that had Texas cousins who mostly never spoke. And then there was the California branch that owned vineyards she'd maybe heard mentioned once. It was insane. The Reynauds had so many branches, so many healthy, thriving parts, and yet they didn't even function as a family. Didn't they know how fortunate they were?

Her phone buzzed on the wrought-iron patio table. An incoming text lit up the screen. She swiped her finger across and found a photo from the night before. A photo of the teenage cancer patient who'd worn the jester hat, her mom and dad leaning in on either side of her with matching smiles.

The text scrolled: We're making memories for a

lifetime with every moment. Thank you for an awesome night!

A second photo came through of the girl with Henri and Jean-Pierre: So excited to meet football idols. She texted the photo to all her school friends. Thank you again.

The joy on the teen's face, on her parents' faces, blew Fiona away. They weren't just brave. Somehow they were happy in the moment. Something her family had never quite managed.

Something she'd never managed.

She'd walked away from her marriage because she didn't know if she could deal with Henri's fears. But had she even tried to manage her own? Could she honestly live with herself if she cut them both off without trying to get a handle on those fears? Her finger traced the faces—genuinely happy faces—and wondered how she'd missed that joy for herself. She kept telling Henri she was strong. But maybe she hadn't been strong enough to truly live in the moment.

It was time to quit assuming Henri would fall apart the way her father had. It was time to stop fearing she would follow her mother's path.

She'd already chosen a different path with her surgery. A hopeful path. She could embrace the day and be her own person, no matter what that future held. It was time to accept the happiness waiting for her.

Snatching up her phone and wallet, she wasn't wasting another moment. She rushed to the closest airport where the family kept their jet. She called Gervais on the way, needing to clear it with him before she used it, but he not only gave his approval, he also managed to put a pilot on site to greet her with the flight plan filed for immediate takeoff. What a godsend to have the support system of family. Why had she spent so much time pushing them away with both hands?

Fiona's stomach was a bundle of nerves as the Gulfstream touched down in Indianapolis. She'd watched the rest of the game on the jet's television, catching the final few plays in a streaming app on her phone.

Henri had been benched even though he stood up after that hard hit in the backfield. He didn't seem to have been treated for concussion symptoms, but maybe they'd say as much in the press to dance around the fact that he simply hadn't played well.

The Hurricanes barely won, and only because the game had been put into the rest of the team's hands while the Bayou Bomber sat one out. Dempsey's strategic coaching had coaxed a win out of the backup quarterback and the rest of the starters, so she suspected Henri wasn't going to be in any kind of mood to see her and talk about their problems.

Again.

But she'd come too far now to back off. And thanks to Gervais's help again, she'd landed at the airport and hopefully would make it to meet them before they left. The jet taxied over to the parking area. She peered out the window, praying she had enough time to get to the stadium. Were any of the parked jets theirs? Surely if they'd left, Gervais would have let the pilot know their flight was in vain.

Just when she was about to grab her phone to call him and check, she caught sight of a chartered bus driving toward one of the other planes. The sort of bus the team would usually travel in collectively to the airport. Her stomach did cartwheels.

Could she have been that close to missing him? Yes, they could have spoken later, but now that she'd figured out what she'd been missing—the happiness she'd been robbing them both of—she couldn't bear the thought of waiting a second longer to see Henri.

Her jet stopped wonderfully close to the path of the bus—bless the pilot and Gervais. Eons later—or at least it felt so—the steps were in place on the Gulf-stream so she could disembark. Cautious feet found purchase on the stairway leading out of the jet. Wind gusting her hair back, she had to bring her hands to her eyes to make out the New Orleans Hurricanes team inside the bus. But then the charter bus's door opened, and the players exited one after the other.

Heart beating hard in her chest, she scanned the team for Henri. Dempsey. Wild Card. Freight Train.

They were all there. But where was Henri?

She felt far away from her body as he came into view. His broad shoulders and wind-tossed dark hair. Sunglasses that shielded his eyes even though night had fallen. Did he see her?

She couldn't wait for him to notice her. Here she was. Ready to gamble, to leap. Gathering her voice, she yelled his name.

She half tripped down the steps of the jet, her ballet flats pounding the asphalt as she ran toward him, still calling out.

"Henri? Henri!" she shouted, her feet picking up pace, her dress wrapping around her legs.

Henri's back was to her now, but his muscular frame was easy to pick out in his tailored charcoal-colored suit.

No matter what he wore, he was still as sexy as the day she'd met him.

He glanced over his shoulder. He cocked his head to the side, then as the distance closed between them she could see him raise an eyebrow. Luckily Dempsey waved away security and Henri broke ranks.

Henri's arms went wide and without hesitation she flew into them. That easy. That right. She was his. He was hers.

He looked over at his brother. "Dempsey, can we have a moment?"

Dempsey laughed. "Now you ask permission?" He gave his brother a shove in Fiona's direction.

Henri took her by the elbow and guided her back into the Reynauds' private jet. "Why are you here? Wait. Never mind. Who the hell cares? You're here."

He hauled her into his arms and kissed her. Really kissed her in a way he hadn't done in…she couldn't remember when. It was something more than the kisses of their early romance. Something more than the kisses of their newlywed days. This was the kiss of a couple tested in fire. More than the fire of passion, but the fire of life.

She eased back, sweeping her hand over his hair that curled after a fresh wash. "I'm here to say I'm sorry. To say I want to try if you'll forgive me for being afraid to face the future. Living in the day was so much…safer."

"God, I lo—"

She pressed a hand to his mouth. "I know. You've

shown me in a million ways with your patience, but I want to be the one to say it first. I love you. I want to spend every day of my life with you. I want to live for each day and focus on that. The joy, the beauty, the art. Our love. And yes, our family. I want to focus on the positive every day for however many days we have." She traced his lips. "I hope you understand that while half the fear was for me, the other half was fear of hurting you."

"Losing you these past months has hurt like hell." His arms found her waist, snaked around her hips. He pulled her closer, as if she'd blow away in the wind if he didn't. She'd missed the feel of his arms around her. Had forgotten what being together—truly together— was like.

"I'm sorry. Who would have thought dreaming of a future would be so scary?"

"I do understand, but you'll help me be strong, won't you?" His smile was light but his dark eyes were serious.

"We'll help each other. I hope there will be countless days. It's not about how much time we have, but how beautiful we can make each day together."

"Not that I'm going to tempt fate here, but I am curious. What made you change your mind? Did my family hound you? Because if they're being pushy just let me know."

"Actually, they've been incredibly helpful. Gervais even set up the plane. Looking back, I'm rethinking our decision to keep them in the dark these past months." She glanced at the window, at the bus full of players waiting patiently as the exhaust puffed into the night air. "I learned my lesson from a photo the mom of one of the patients at the party texted me. I can show you later. It's…beautiful."

"I look forward to seeing it." He brushed a kiss across her lips. "I want us to talk more, share more, spend more time together. I've decided I should quit the team."

Shock pulled at her heartstrings. She had to have misheard him. Football wasn't just a job for him. Passion for the game ran as deep as her passion for art. "What?"

"At the end of the season, I'm through."

"What about your contract?" Another gust of fall wind ripped past them, carrying the smell of oil and decomposing leaves past them.

Pushing the hair from her eyes, he kissed her forehead, his lips gentle and warm in the cool atmosphere.

"I'll buy out. Money's not an issue."

"You love the game. I don't understand." Fiona shook her head, processing the logic of his words.

"I love you more, and I'll do whatever it takes to win you back. We'll take more time to get to know each other, at home or traveling, or starting a fund-raising foundation. I'm committed to making this work. No half measures. I want you as my wife, my love, my life." He spoke in earnest. She could see that in the way a faint smile tugged at the corner of his lips and how his gaze intensified as he stared into her eyes.

But Henri without football? That didn't seem right. The game twined with his soul, his purpose. They had to reach a point where they accepted all of each other, no holding back, no reservations. They couldn't pick and choose parts to love and parts to neglect. That road had led them to ruin.

Time to begin again. To take bigger chances and risks together.

She rested her head against his chest, listening to his pounding heart. He offered her complete devotion and she appreciated the sentiment, needed to hear he'd move heaven and earth for them. But she didn't need Henri to give up his job to fix them. They'd do that together.

"Henri, you don't have to give up your job for me."

"I do if it means I could lose you again."

She repeated her thoughts from earlier out loud. "I'm yours. You're mine. When I talk about the joy of living, I mean embracing every part of who we are. I love the game, traveling, seeing you play. We can figure out the details together. If we need to, we can truly talk with the counselor rather than racing straight to the lawyer. Are you okay with that?" Communication. That's what they needed. Old-fashioned communication.

"Whatever it takes. I've made that clear." He kissed her nose. Her temple. Her neck. Her mouth. Each kiss affirming his commitment—a promise imprinted into her skin. Into her soul.

Enjoying the feel of him, she asked, "What if I say counseling and you keep playing?"

Her fingers traced designs on the back of his neck as their eyes met.

"I think you're letting me off too easily, my love."

She rolled her eyes and arched up to give him a quick kiss. "Oh, I don't think this is going to be easy at all. Not if we dig in deep with counseling."

"I can face it if we're together." He intertwined their hands. Raised their joined fists to his lips. Kissed the back of her hand while staring into her eyes.

"Together, as a team." She stepped closer, their clasped hands against her heart. "That sounds like a winning game plan to me."

* * * * *

If you loved this novel,
pick up all the books in the
BAYOU BILLIONAIRES series
from USA TODAY bestselling author
Catherine Mann
and
Joanne Rock

HIS PREGNANT PRINCESS BRIDE
by Catherine Mann
HIS SECRETARY'S SURPRISE FIANCÉ
by Joanne Rock
REUNITED WITH THE REBEL BILLIONAIRE
by Catherine Mann

and

SECRET BABY SCANDAL by Joanne Rock
Available May 2016!

Only from Harlequin Desire.

***

Read on for an exclusive sneak preview of
ONE NIGHT CHARMER
from USA TODAY bestselling author Maisey Yates
and HQN Books.

***

If you're on Twitter, tell us what you think of
Harlequin Desire! #harlequindesire

*Copper Ridge, Oregon's favorite bachelor
is about to meet his match!*

*If the devil wore flannel, he'd look like Ace
Thompson. He's gruff. Opinionated. Infernally hot.
The last person Sierra West wants to ask for a
bartending job—not that she has a choice. Ever
since discovering that her "perfect" family is built
on a lie, Sierra has been determined to make it
on her own. Resisting her new boss should be
easy when they're always bickering. Until one
night, the squabbling stops...and something
far more dangerous takes over.*

Ace has a personal policy against messing around
with staff—or with spoiled rich girls. But there's
a steel backbone beneath Sierra's silver-spoon
upbringing. She's tougher than he thought, and
so much more tempting. Enough to make him
want to break all his rules, even if it means
risking his heart...

Read on for this special extended excerpt from
ONE NIGHT CHARMER
by USA TODAY *bestselling author Maisey Yates.*

CHAPTER ONE

THERE WERE TWO people in Copper Ridge, Oregon, who—between them—knew nearly every secret of every person in town. The first was Pastor John Thompson, who heard confessions of sin and listened to people pour out their hearts when they were going through trials and tribulations.

The second was Ace Thompson, owner of the most popular bar in town, son of the pastor and probably the least likely to attend church on Sunday or any other day.

There was no question that his father knew a lot of secrets, though Ace was pretty certain he himself got the more honest version. His father spent time standing behind the pulpit; Ace stood behind a bar. And there he learned the deepest and darkest situations happening in the lives of other townspeople while never revealing any of his own. He supposed, pastor or bartender, that was kind of the perk.

They poured it all out for you, and you got to keep your secrets bottled up inside.

That was how Ace liked it. Every night of the week, he had the best seat in the house for whatever show Copper Ridge wanted to put on. And he didn't even have to pay for it.

And with his newest acquisition, the show was about to get a whole lot better.

"Really?" Jack Monaghan sat down at the bar, beer in hand, his arm around his new fiancée, Kate Garrett. "A mechanical bull?"

"That's right, Monaghan. This is a classy establishment, after all."

"Seriously," Connor Garrett said, taking the seat next to Jack, followed by his wife, Liss. "Where did you get that thing?"

"I traded it. Guy down in Tolowa owed me some money and he didn't have it. So he said I could come by and look at his stash of trash. Lo and behold, I discovered Ferdinand over there."

"Congratulations," Kate said. "I didn't think anything could make this place more of a dive. I was wrong."

"You're a peach, Kate," Ace said.

The woman smiled broadly and wrapped her arm around Jack's, leaning in and resting her cheek on his shoulder.

"Can we get a round?" Connor asked.

Ace continued to listen to their conversation as he served up their usual brew, enjoying the happy tenor of the conversation, since the downers would probably be around later to dish out woe while he served up harder liquor. The Garretts were good people, he mused. Always had been. Both before he'd left Copper Ridge, and since he'd come back.

His focus was momentarily pulled away when the pretty blonde who'd been hanging out in the dining room all evening drinking with friends approached the aforementioned Ferdinand.

He hadn't had too many people ride the bull yet, and he had to admit, he was finding it a pretty damn enjoyable novelty.

The woman tossed her head, her tan cowboy hat staying in place while her blond curls went wild around her shoulders. She wrapped her hands around the harness on top of the mechanical creature and hoisted herself up. Her movements were unsteady, and he had a feeling, based on the amount of time the group had been here, and how often the men in the group had come and gone from the bar, that she was more than a little bit tipsy.

Best seat in the house. He always had the best seat in the house.

She glanced up as she situated herself and he got a good look at her face. There was a determined glint in her eyes, her brows locked together, her lips pursed into a tight circle. She wasn't just tipsy, she was pissed. Looking down at the bull like it was her own personal Everest and she was determined to conquer it along with her rage. He wondered what a bedazzled little thing like her had to be angry about. A broken nail, maybe. A pair of shoes that she really wanted that was unavailable in her size.

She nodded once, her expression growing even *more* determined as she signaled the employee Ace had operating the controls tonight.

Ace moved nearer to the bar, planting his hands flat on the surface. "This probably won't end well."

The patrons at the bar turned their heads toward the scene. And he noticed Jack's posture go rigid. "Is that—"

"Yes," Kate said.

The mechanical bull pitched forward and the petite blonde sitting on top of it pitched right along with it. She managed to stay seated, but in Ace's opinion that was a miracle. The bull went back again, and the woman straightened, arching her back and thrusting her breasts forward, her head tilted upward, the overhead lighting bathing her pretty face in a golden glow. And for a moment, just a moment, she looked like a graceful, dirty angel getting into the rhythm of the kind of riding Ace preferred above anything else.

Then the great automated beast pitched forward again and the little lady went over the top, down onto the mats underneath. There were howls from her so-called friends as they enjoyed her deposition just a little too much.

She stood on shaky legs and walked back over to the group, picking up a shot glass and tossing back another, her face twisted into an expression that suggested this was not typical behavior for her.

Kate frowned and got up from her stool, making her way over to the other woman.

Ace had a feeling he should know the woman's name, had a feeling that he probably did somewhere in the back corner of his mind. He knew everyone. Which meant that he knew a lot *about* a lot of people, recognized nearly every face he passed on the street. He could usually place them with their most defining life moments, as those were the things that often spilled out on the bar top after a few shots too many.

But it didn't mean he could put a name to every face. There were simply too many of them.

"Who is that?" he asked.

"Sierra West," Jack said, something strange in his tone.

"Oh, right."

He knew the West family well enough, or rather,

he knew of them. Everyone did. Though they were hardly the type to frequent his establishment. Sierra did, which would explain why she was familiar, though they never made much in the way of conversation. She was the type who was always absorbed in her friends or her cell phone when she came to place her order. No deep confessionals from Sierra over drinks.

He'd always found it a little strange she patronized his bar when the rest of the West family didn't.

Dive bars weren't really their thing.

He imagined mechanical bulls probably weren't, either. Judging not just on Sierra's pedigree, but on the poor performance.

"No cotillions going on tonight, I guess," Ace said.

Jack turned his head sharply, his expression dark. "What's that supposed to mean?"

"Nothing."

He didn't know why, but his statement had clearly offended Monaghan. Ace wasn't in the business of voicing his opinion. He was in the business of listening. Listening and serving. No one needed to know his take on a damn thing. They just wanted a sounding board to voice their own opinions and hear them echoed back.

Typically, he had no trouble with that. This had been a little slipup.

"She's not so bad," Jack said.

Sierra was a friend of Jack's fiancée, that much was obvious. Kate was over there talking to her, expression concerned. Sierra still looked mutinous. Ace was starting to wonder if she was mad at the entire world, or if something in particular had set her off.

"I'm sure she isn't." He wasn't sure of any such

thing. In fact, if he knew one thing about the world and all the people in it, it was that there was a particular type who used their every advantage in life to take whatever they wanted, whenever they wanted it, regardless of promises made. Whether they were words whispered in the dark or vows spoken in front of whole crowds of loved ones.

He was a betting man. And he would lay odds that Sierra West was one of those people. She was the type. Rich, a big fish in the small pond of the community and beautiful. That combination pretty much guaranteed her whatever she wanted. And when the option for *whatever you wanted* was available, very few people resisted it.

Hell, why would you? There were a host of things he would change if he had infinite money and power.

But just because he figured he'd be in the same boat if he were rich and almighty didn't mean he had to like it on others.

He looked back over at Kate, who patted her friend on the shoulder before shaking her head and walking back toward the group. "She didn't want to come sit with us or anything," Kate said, looking frustrated.

The Garrett-Monaghan crew lingered at the bar for another couple of hours before they were replaced by another set of customers. Sierra's group thinned out a little bit, but didn't disperse completely. A couple of the guys were starting to get rowdy, and Ace was starting to think he was going to have to play the part of his own bouncer tonight. It wouldn't be the first time.

Fortunately, the noisier members of the group slowly trickled outside. He watched as Sierra got up and made her way back to the bathroom, leaving a couple of girls—one of whom he assumed was the designated driver—sitting at the table.

The tab was caught up, so he didn't really care how it all went down. He wasn't a babysitter, after all.

He turned, grabbed a rag out of the bucket beneath the counter and started to wipe it down. When he looked up again, the girls who had been sitting at the table were gone, and Sierra West was standing in the center of the room looking around like she was lost.

Then she glanced his way, and her eyes lit up like a sinner looking at salvation.

Wrong guess, honey.

She wandered over to the bar, her feet unsteady. "Did you see where my friends went?"

She had that look about her. Like a lost baby deer. All wide, dewy eyes and unsteady limbs. And damned if she wasn't cute as hell.

"Out the door," he said, almost feeling sorry for her. Almost.

She wasn't the first pretty young drunk to get ditched in his bar by stupid friends. She was also exactly the kind of woman he avoided at all costs, no matter how cute or seemingly vulnerable she was.

"What?" She swayed slightly. "They weren't supposed to leave me."

She sounded mystified. Completely dumbfounded that anyone would ever leave her high and dry.

"I figured," he said. "Here's a tip—get better friends."

She frowned. "They're the best friends I have."

He snorted. "That's a sad story."

She held up her hand, the broad gesture out of place coming from such a refined creature. "Just a second."

"Sure."

She turned away, heading toward the door and out to the parking lot.

He swore. He didn't know if she had a car out there, but she was way too skunked to drive.

"Watch the place, Jenna," he said to one of the waitresses, who nodded and assumed a rather important-looking position with her hands flat on the bar and a rag in her hand, as though she were ready to wipe crumbs away with serious authority.

He rounded the counter and followed the same path Sierra had just taken out into the parking lot. He looked around for a moment and didn't see her. Then he looked down and there she was, sitting on the edge of the curb. "Everything okay?"

That was a stupid question; he already knew the answer.

She looked up. "No."

He let out a long-drawn-out sigh. The problem was, he'd followed her out here. If he had just let her walk out the door, then nothing but the pine trees and the seagulls would have been responsible for her. But no, he'd had to follow. He'd been concerned about her driving. And now he would have to follow through on that concern.

"You don't have a ride?"

She shook her head, looking miserable. "Everyone left me. Because they aren't nice. You're right. I do need better friends."

"Yes," he said, "you do. And let me go ahead and tell you right now, I won't be one of them. But as long as you don't live somewhere ridiculous like Portland, I can give you a ride home."

And this, right here, was the curse of owning a bar. Whether he should or not, he felt responsible in these situations. She was compromised, it was late, and she was alone. He could not let her meander her way back home. Not when he could easily see that she got there safely.

"A ride?" She frowned, her delicate features lit dramatically by the security light hanging on the front of the bar.

"I know your daddy probably told you not to take rides from strangers, but trust me, I'm the safest bet around. Unless you want to call someone." He checked his watch. "It's inching close to last call. I'm betting not very many people are going to come out right now."

She shook her head slowly. "Probably not."

He sighed heavily, reaching into his pocket and wrapping his fingers around his keys. "All right, come on. Get in the truck."

SIERRA LOOKED UP at her unlikely, bearded, plaid-clad savior. She knew who he was, of course. Ace Thompson was the owner of the bar, and she bought beer from him at least twice a month when she came out with her friends. They'd exchanged money and drinks across the counter more times than she could recall, but this was more words than she'd ever exchanged with him in her life.

She was angry at herself. For getting drunk. For going out with the biggest jerks in the local rodeo club. For getting on the back of a mechanical bull and opening herself up to their derision—because honestly, when you put your drunk self up on a fake, bucking animal, you pretty much deserved it. And most of all, for sitting down in the parking lot acting like she was going to cry just because she had been ditched by said jerky friends.

Oh, and being *caught* at what was most definitely an epic low made it all even worse. He'd almost certainly seen her inglorious dismount off the mechanical bull, then witnessed everyone leaving without her.

She'd been so sure today couldn't get any worse.

She'd been wrong.

"I'm fine," she said, and she could have bitten off her own tongue, because she wasn't fine. As much as she wanted to pretend she didn't need his help, she kind of did. Granted, she could call Colton or Madison. But if her sister had to drive all the way down to town from the family estate she would probably kill Sierra. And if she called Colton's house his fiancée would probably kill Sierra.

Either way, that made for a dead Sierra.

She wasn't speaking to her father. Which, really, was the root of today's evil.

"Sure you are. *Most* girls who end up sitting on their behinds at 1:00 a.m. in a parking lot are just fine."

She blinked, trying to bring his face into focus. He refused to be anything but a fuzzy blur. "I am."

For some reason, her stubbornness was on full display, and most definitely outweighed her common sense. That was probably related to the alcohol. And to the fact that all of her restraint had been torn down hours ago. Sometime early this morning when she had screamed at her father and told him she never wanted to see him again, because she'd found out he was a liar. A cheater.

Right, so that was probably why she was feeling rebellious. Angry in general. But she probably shouldn't direct it at the person who was offering a helping hand.

"Don't make me ask you twice, Sierra. It's going to make me get real grumpy, and I don't think you'll like that." Ace shifted his stance, crossing his arms over his broad chest—she was pretty sure it was broad, either that or she was seeing double—and looked down at her.

She got to her wobbly feet, pitching slightly to the side before steadying herself. Her head was spinning, her stomach churning, and she was just mad. Because she felt like crap. Because she knew better than to drink like this, at least when she wasn't in the privacy of her own home.

"Which truck?" she asked, rubbing her forehead.

He turned, not waiting for her, and began to walk across the parking lot. She followed as quickly as she could. Fortunately, the lot was mostly empty, so she didn't have to watch much but the back of Ace as they made their way to the vehicle. It wasn't a new, flashy truck. It was old, but it was in good condition. Better than most she'd seen at such an advanced age. But then, Ace wasn't a rancher. He owned a bar, so it wasn't like his truck saw all that much action.

She stood in front of the passenger-side door for a long moment before realizing he was not coming around to open it for her. Her face heated as she jerked open the door for herself and climbed up inside.

It had a bench seat. And she found herself clinging to the door, doing her best to keep the expansive seat between them as wide as possible. She was suddenly conscious of the fact that he was a very large man. Tall, broad, muscular. She'd known that, somewhere in the back of her mind. But the way he filled up the cab of a truck containing just the two of them was much more significant than the way he filled the space in a vast and crowded bar.

He started the engine, saying nothing as he put the truck in Reverse and began to pull out of the lot. She looked straight ahead, desperate to find something to say. The silence was oppressive, heavy around them. It made her feel twitchy, nervous. She always knew what to say. She was in command of every social situation she stepped into. People found her charming, and if they didn't, they never said otherwise. Because she was Sierra West, and her family name carried with it the burden of mandatory respect from the people of Copper Ridge.

She took a deep breath, trying to ease the pressure in her chest, trying to remove the weight that was sitting there.

"What's your sign?" Somehow, her fuzzy brain had retrieved that as a conversation starter. The moment the words left her mouth she wanted to stuff them back in and swallow them.

To her surprise, he laughed. "Caution."

"What?"

"I'm a caution sign, baby. And it would be in your best interest to obey the warning…"

*Don't miss what happens when Sierra
doesn't heed his advice in
ONE NIGHT CHARMER
by* USA TODAY *bestselling author Maisey Yates.*

REQUEST YOUR FREE BOOKS!
2 FREE NOVELS PLUS 2 FREE GIFTS!

H HARLEQUIN®

Desire

ALWAYS POWERFUL, PASSIONATE AND PROVOCATIVE

YES! Please send me 2 FREE Harlequin® Desire novels and my 2 FREE gifts (gifts are worth about $10). After receiving them, if I don't wish to receive any more books, I can return the shipping statement marked "cancel." If I don't cancel, I will receive 6 brand-new novels every month and be billed just $4.55 per book in the U.S. or $5.24 per book in Canada. That's a savings of at least 13% off the cover price! It's quite a bargain! Shipping and handling is just 50¢ per book in the U.S. and 75¢ per book in Canada.* I understand that accepting the 2 free books and gifts places me under no obligation to buy anything. I can always return a shipment and cancel at any time. Even if I never buy another book, the two free books and gifts are mine to keep forever.

225/326 HDN GH2P

Name _____ (PLEASE PRINT) _____

Address _____ Apt. # _____

City _____ State/Prov. _____ Zip/Postal Code _____

Signature (if under 18, a parent or guardian must sign)

Mail to the **Reader Service:**
IN U.S.A.: P.O. Box 1867, Buffalo, NY 14240-1867
IN CANADA: P.O. Box 609, Fort Erie, Ontario L2A 5X3

Want to try two free books from another line?
Call 1-800-873-8635 or visit www.ReaderService.com.

* Terms and prices subject to change without notice. Prices do not include applicable taxes. Sales tax applicable in N.Y. Canadian residents will be charged applicable taxes. Offer not valid in Quebec. This offer is limited to one order per household. Not valid for current subscribers to Harlequin Desire books. All orders subject to credit approval. Credit or debit balances in a customer's account(s) may be offset by any other outstanding balance owed by or to the customer. Please allow 4 to 6 weeks for delivery. Offer available while quantities last.

Your Privacy—The Reader Service is committed to protecting your privacy. Our Privacy Policy is available online at www.ReaderService.com or upon request from the Reader Service.

We make a portion of our mailing list available to reputable third parties that offer products we believe may interest you. If you prefer that we not exchange your name with third parties, or if you wish to clarify or modify your communication preferences, please visit us at www.ReaderService.com/consumerschoice or write to us at Reader Service Preference Service, P.O. Box 9062, Buffalo, NY 14240-9062. Include your complete name and address.

HDI5

Grateful to have made it without getting lost, Brooke had
to contend with the fact she was *here*. And now, one way
or another, her life was going to change forever. She rang
the doorbell. A moment later, she stood face-to-face with
Wyatt.

Who was holding a squirming baby boy.

It was the last thing she expected.

"Wyatt?" She was rendered speechless, staring at the
man who'd made her insides quiver just one month ago.

"Come in, Brooke. I'm glad you made it."

She stared at him, still not believing what she was
seeing. He'd never mentioned having a child. Although,
there'd seemed to be a silent agreement between them
not to delve too deeply into their private lives.

She stepped inside and Wyatt closed the door behind
her. "This is Brett, my son. He was supposed to be

sleeping by the time you arrived. Obviously that didn't happen. Babies tend to make liars of their parents, and it's been rough without a nanny."

"He's beautiful."

"Thanks, he's the best part of me. Well, him and his twin, Brianna."

"There's two of them?"

"I want to explain. Why don't you have a seat?" He started walking and she followed. "You look pretty, by the way," he said, his cowboy charm taking hold again, and she had trouble remembering how he'd dumped her after a spectacular night of sex.

A night when they'd conceived a child.

"You didn't tell me you had children."

"I just wanted to be me—not a father, not a widower—that night. My friends are forever saying I need to find myself again. That's what I was trying to do."

She inhaled a sharp breath, everything becoming clear.

If she were brave, she'd reveal her pregnancy to Wyatt and try to cope with the decisions they would make together. But her courage failed her. How could she tell this widower with twins he was about to be a father again?

Don't miss
TWINS FOR THE TEXAN
by USA TODAY *bestselling author Charlene Sands*
available May 2016 wherever
Harlequin® Desire books and ebooks are sold.

www.Harlequin.com

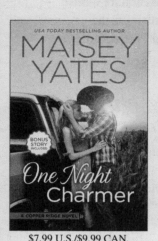

USA TODAY BESTSELLING AUTHOR
MAISEY YATES

One Night
Charmer

A COPPER RIDGE NOVEL

BONUS STORY INCLUDED

$7.99 U.S./$9.99 CAN.

EXCLUSIVE
Limited time offer!

$1.⁰⁰ OFF

USA TODAY Bestselling Author
MAISEY YATES

Copper Ridge, Oregon's favorite
bachelor is about to meet his match in

One Night
Charmer

Available April 19, 2016.
Pick up your copy today!

HQN™

$1.⁰⁰ OFF   the purchase price of
ONE NIGHT CHARMER by Maisey Yates.

Offer valid from April 19, 2016, to May 31, 2016. Redeemable at participating retail
outlets. Not redeemable at Barnes & Noble. Limit one coupon per purchase.
Valid in the U.S.A. and Canada only.

52613441

5 65373 00076 2   (8100)0 12138

PHMY0516COUP

Looking for more passionate reads?
Collect these stories from
Harlequin Presents and Harlequin Blaze!

HARLEQUIN *Presents*

MORELLI'S MISTRESS
by *USA TODAY* bestselling author Anne Mather

Luke Morelli is back and determined that Abby Laurence
will pay for her past betrayal. Finally free of her husband,
there's only one way she can make amends... Their affair
was once illicit, but she's Luke's for the taking now!

HARLEQUIN *Blaze*

DARING HER SEAL
(Uniformly Hot!)
by *New York Times* bestselling author Anne Marsh

DEA agent Ashley Dixon and Navy SEAL Levi Brandon
are shocked to discover their faux wedding from their last
mission was legitimate. They don't even like each other!
Which doesn't mean they aren't hot for each other...

Available wherever books and ebooks are sold.

HPB0416

THE WORLD IS BETTER WITH

Romance

Harlequin has everything from contemporary, passionate and heartwarming to suspenseful and inspirational stories.

Whatever your mood, we have a romance just for you!

Connect with us to find your next great read, special offers and more.

f /HarlequinBooks

🐦 @HarlequinBooks

www.HarlequinBlog.com

www.Harlequin.com/Newsletters

A *Romance* FOR EVERY MOOD™

www.Harlequin.com

SERIESHALOAD2015